Originally published in London by A. Bettesworth, 1723

The original text of *The Life of Charlotta Du Pont* by Penelope Aubin is in the public domain in the United States and worldwide.

Editor's Foreword copyright © 2025 by Jonathan Pezza

This edition copyright © 2025 by Knightsville Workshop

All rights reserved. No part of this publication may be reproduced, distributed, or transmitted in any form or by any means, including photocopying, recording, or other electronic or mechanical methods, without the prior written permission of the publisher, except as permitted by U.S. copyright law.

First Knightsville Workshop edition 2025

ISBN: 979-8-89778-289-5

E-Book ISBN: 979-8-89778-284-0

Cover design by Jonathan Pezza

Printed in the United States of America

EDITOR'S FORWARD

My journey to Penelope Aubin began, somewhat improbably, with pirates.

As a creator, writer, and podcaster who has spent the better part of two decades in the entertainment industry, from editing major studio films to producing the award-winning Curious Matter Anthology podcast, I have always been drawn to stories that challenge conventional narratives.

I am by no means an expert in literary history. I prefer to think of myself as an explorer who believes much of our historical and story-telling record is beginning to slip away into oblivion as our digital present churns out regurgitative and ephemeral content that acts as an echo chamber for an ever-shrinking number of mainstream IPs. What's worse is that this new "content" is meant to disappear as soon as it ceases to generate "clicks," and then erases itself from the digital record, as we have seen time and time again over the last 25 years of the digital media landscape. As physical media becomes less and less utilized, it comes down to us, the independent creators, to reconstruct and preserve our own history and the legacies of the creators on whose shoulders we now stand.

And as such, I would like to present a writer who helped birth the romance and adventure genres and the very art of novel writing itself, the incredible Mrs. Penelope Aubin.

When I embarked on what I call "The Pirate Project" in 2020, a comprehensive multimedia investigation into the Golden Age of Piracy using twenty-first-century forensic technologies and the constantly expanding digital record, I hoped to uncover new evidence about the lives of legendary figures like Anne Bonny and Mary Read. What I did not expect was to discover an entire literary ecosystem that has been hiding in plain sight for three centuries.

As I was researching the publishing industry of 1720s London, I discovered that the same decade that witnessed the height of Caribbean piracy was the same that gave birth to the modern English novel, driven in large part by a cohort of pioneering women writers whose contributions have been systematically marginalized by traditional literary history. The same popular fascination with piracy that filled London taverns with tales of adventure and rebellion was simultaneously filling London's bookshops with novels by authors like Eliza Haywood, Delarivier Manley, and Penelope Aubin, women who were not merely reflecting contemporary culture but actively reshaping it.

The 1720s represented the convergence of literary innovation, commercial opportunity, and social transformation. The lapse of the Licensing Act in 1695 had unleashed an unprecedented flowering of free press and publishing activity. By 1720, London supported a thriving network of booksellers, circulating libraries, and literary periodicals that created, for the first time in English history, a truly commercial marketplace for fiction. Beyond this, I had not realized that female authors had more than established their presence in the literary marketplace," accounting for a significant percentage of all published works, but were central to establishing the industry. This was the decade when the novel as we know it was being invented— not by the traditionally celebrated triumvirate of Defoe, Richardson, and Fielding, but by a diverse community of writers experimenting with new forms of storytelling that combined moral instruction with popular entertainment.

Mrs. Aubin stands at the center of this revolution. Between 1721 and 1728, she published seven novels that captured the contemporary fascination with exotic adventure while pioneering narrative techniques that would influence generations of writers. Her works featured what modern scholars have described as "kick-ass teenage girls"—resourceful heroines who navigated global adventures from the Caribbean to the Mediterranean, defending their virtue and their lives through courage, intelligence, and what Aubin consistently portrayed as divine providence. These were not passive victims of male oppression but active agents of their own destinies. These characters subverted the highly restrictive gender roles of their time while maintaining the moral respectability that allowed female authors to reach mainstream audiences.

The Life of Charlotta Du Pont, published in 1723, exemplifies Aubin's revolutionary approach to fiction. The novel's complex narrative structure of weaveing together multiple storylines and perspectives, establishes the sophisticated literary techniques that would later be associated with more celebrated authors. But more importantly, it presents a template for what we might call "virtuous rebellion"—a model for how women might live adventurous, autonomous lives outside the confines of traditional domestic roles while maintaining their moral authority and social standing.

This was not merely literary innovation but cultural intervention. Aubin and her contemporaries were creating what scholars now recognize as "the rich tradition of early fiction by women"—works that "pared the seduction plot away from the political focus" of earlier women writers, to focus their texts on a woman's response to sexual experience and betrayal." They established patterns of female characterization and moral instruction that would prove "particularly relevant to the work of Richardson" and other later novelists who would receive greater historical recognition.

The broader landscape of 1720s novel writing reveals a literary ecosystem far more diverse and dynamic than traditional literary histories acknowledge. Alongside Aubin, writers like Eliza Haywood were achieving remarkable commercial success—Haywood's Love in

Excess (1719) "came out the same year as Daniel Defoe's Robinson Crusoe" and enjoyed "a similar level of popularity and notoriety." Mary Davys, Elizabeth Rowe, and others were experimenting with new ideas of romance and adventure fiction, each contributing to what would become the foundation of the modern novel.

These writers created the essential building blocks of romance and adventure fiction that would enable later authors like Jane Austen to flourish. They established the novel as a legitimate literary art form, developed original techniques for psychological characterization on a moral foundation, and proved that fiction could be both entertaining and edifying. They demonstrated that women could be professional authors, that novels could address serious social issues, and that popular literature could achieve both commercial success and critical respectability.

Perhaps most importantly, they created new models of female agency and adventure that expanded the possibilities for how women's lives could be imagined and lived. Through virtue, unbreakable spirit, and faith in divine justice, Aubin's heroines carved out spaces of freedom and self-determination that challenged the misogynistic constraints of their historical moment while pointing toward more expansive futures.

Recovering these voices is not merely an act of historical justice but an essential corrective to our understanding of literary development. As we continue to discover new evidence through digital archives and forensic research methods—the same twenty-first-century technologies I employ in The Pirate Project—it becomes increasingly clear that the traditional narrative of the novel's origins needs fundamental revision. The earliest entries in the English fiction landscape were laid not just by a few celebrated men but by a diverse community of innovators who created the forms and conventions that would define literature for centuries to come.

The Life of Charlotta Du Pont deserves recognition not only as an entertaining adventure story but as a crucial document in the history of women's writing and the development of the English novel. In returning this work to print, we restore not just a lost book but a lost world—one in which women writers were central figures in the creation of modern literature, and in which the spirit of adventure and the pursuit of virtue were seen not as contradictory but as complementary paths toward human flourishing. These pioneering female writers balked the norms of their time, and charted new territories. Their legacy lives on not only in the novels they wrote but in the possibilities they opened for all the writers who would follow.

Honoring that contribution, I have presented this new edition of the novel in a way that preserves the language and prose, while making subtle adjustments to improve readability of archaic abbreviations, spelling, paragraph separation, and capitalization. This presentation of the novel is an entirely new transcription of the text from the 1st edition scans. My hope is that these minor adjustments to the original text and attention to detail in designing this new edition will help new audiences discover this work as I have, for generations to come.

Jonathan Pezza
Los Angeles, 2025

THE
LIFE
OF
Charlotta Du Pont,
An English Lady,
Taken from her own memoirs.

A History that contains the greatest Variety of Events that ever was published.

By Penelope Aubin

CONTENTS

TO

My much honoured Friend

Mrs. ROWE.

MADAM,

I have long waited for an opportunity to give some public testimony of the esteem and respect I have for you. The friendship you and Mr. Rowe have shown to me and my dead friend has laid me under the greatest obligations to love and value you, but your particular merit has doubly engaged me to honour you. In you, I have found all that is valuable in our sex; and without flattery, you are the best Wife, the best Friend, the most prudent, most humble, and most accomplished woman I ever met withal. I am charmed with your conversation, and extremely proud of your friendship. The world has often condemned me for being too curious, and, as they term it, partial in my Friendships; but I am of a sound mind and take no pleasure in the variety of acquaintance and conversation. Two or three persons of worth and integrity are enough to make life pleasant. I confess I have little to recommend me to such, except the grateful sense I have of the honor they do me, and the love I bear their virtues; and I account it my good Fortune to have found such friends, amongst whom I esteem you in the first rank. I need say nothing of Mr. Rowe, but that he has such excellencies as prevailed with you, who are an admirable judge, and endowed with as much sense and virtue as any woman living, to prefer him before all the rest of mankind: and your choice is sufficient to speak his merit. May heaven prolong your lives, and continue your felicity, that your friends may long enjoy you, and the world be bettered by your examples. You act as your learned father taught (Dr. Barker, Dean of Exeter), and are in all kinds an honour to the ancient noble families from whence you are descended. Forgive this rapture, my zeal transports me when you are the subject of my thoughts, and I had almost forgot to entreat the favour of you to accept the little present I here make of the adventures of a lady, whose life was full of the most extraordinary incidents. I hope it will agreeably entertain you at a leisure hour, and I assure you I dedicate it to you with the utmost respect and affection, and am, madam,

Your most sincere friend, and devoted humble servant,

Penelope Aubin.

PREFACE

Gentlemen and Ladies,

The court being removed to the other side of the water, and beyond sea, to take the pleasures this town and our dull island cannot afford; the greater part of our nobility and members of Parliament retired to Hanover or their country-seats, where they may supinely sit, and with pleasure reflect on the great things they have done for the public good, and the mighty toils they have sustained from sultry days and sleepless nights, unraveling the horrid plot: whilst these our great patriots enjoy the repose of their own consciences, and reap the fruits of their labors, and enlarged prisoners freed from stone walls, and jailers taste the sweets of liberty; I believed something new and diverting would be welcome to the town, and that the adventures of a young lady, whose life contains the most extraordinary events that I ever heard or read of, might agreeably entertain you at a time when our news-papers furnish nothing of moment. The story of Madam Charlotta du Pont, I had from the mouth of a gentleman of integrity, who related it as from his own knowledge. I have joined some other histories to hers, to embellish and render it more entertaining and useful, to encourage virtue, and excite us to heroic actions, which is my principal aim in all I write; and this I hope you will rather applaud than condemn me for. The kind reception you have already given the trifles I have published lays me under an obligation to do something more to merit your favor. Besides, as I am neither a statesman, courtier, nor modern great man or lady, I cannot break my word without blushing, having ever kept it as a thing that is sacred, and I remember I promised in my preface to the Count de Vineville, to continue writing if you dealt favorably with me. My booksellers say my novels sell tolerably well. I had designed to employ my pen on something more serious and learned, but they tell me I shall meet with no encouragement, and advise me to write rather more modishly, that is, less like a Christian, and in a style careless and loose, as the custom of the present age is to live. But I leave that to the other female authors, my contemporaries, whose lives and writings have, I fear, too great a resemblance. My design in writing is to employ my leisure hours to some advantage to myself and others; and I shall forbear publishing any work of greater price and value than these, till times mend, and money again is plenty in England. Necessity may make wits, but authors will be at a loss for patrons and subscribers whilst the nation is poor. I do not write for bread, nor am I vain or fond of applause, but I am very ambitious to gain the esteem of those who honor virtue, and shall ever be

Their devoted humble servant,
Penelope Aubin

CHAPTER 1

Towards the end of King Charles the Second's reign, when a long continuance of peace, and his merciful government, had made our nation the most rich and happy country in the world; a French gentleman, whose name was Monsieur du Pont, being a Protestant, left France, and came and settled near Bristol with his wife. He had been master of a vessel, with which, making many prosperous voyages to the West-Indies, and other places, he had gained a competent estate; and was now resolved to sit down in quiet and pass the remainder of his life at ease, in a country where he might enjoy his religion without molestation. Having disposed of all he had in France, and remitted the money by bills into England, to some merchants his correspondents here, he chose to settle near this sea-port, where he had some acquaintance with the most considerable merchants, with whom he had traded; having been several times in England before, and perfectly skilled in our language.

He put part of his money into the public funds, and with the rest purchased a house and some land, on which he lived with his wife, and some servants, as happily as any man on Earth could do; and nothing was wanting but children to make him completely blessed. He had been married eight years, and had no child; but he had not lived in this healthful country above two years, when his lady with much joy told him, she was with child; at which news he returned thanks to heaven with transport, and she was at the expiration of her time happily delivered of a daughter, whose life is the subject of this history, being full of such strange misfortunes, and wonderful adventures, that it well deserves to be published. They gave her the name of her fond mother, Charlotta, and the child was so beautiful that everybody who saw her admired her.

It's needless to tell you that Monsieur du Pont and his lady bred her up with all the care and tenderness imaginable, But it pleased God to deprive this little creature of her dear mother before she was five years old, for Madam du Pont fell sick of a fever, and died. And now Charlotta was left to her father's care, who, deeply concerned for his lady's death, looked on her as the dear pledge which was left him, of their mutual affection; and was so doatingly fond of her, that he resolved never to marry again, but to make it the business of his life to educate and provide for her, in the most advantageous manner he was able.

The child was beautiful and ingenious, and showed so great a capacity, and so quick an apprehension in all she went about, that he had reason to hope great things from her. Nor were his expectations frustrated; for before she was ten years old, she could play upon the lute and harpsichord, danced finely, spoke French and Latin perfectly, sang ravishingly, wrote delicately, and used her needle with as much art and skill as if Pallas had been her mistress. Monsieur du Pont blessed heaven hourly for her, and delighted in her more than he indeed ought to have done, fancying he could not outlive the loss of her. She was so obedient to his will that his commands were always obeyed, and she never once offended him.

BUT MAN IS A FRAIL CREATURE, and there are unlucky hours in life, which, if not carefully armed against, give us opportunities of being undone. A merchant of London, in whose hands Monsieur du Pont had a great sum of money, died, and he was obliged to make a journey to town, to look after it, and get it out of the executrix's hands, who was looked upon to be no very honest woman. He would not venture to take Charlotta with him, for fear she should be disordered with the journey, or get the smallpox, which she had not as yet had; so he left her with a discreet gentlewoman, whom he had taken into his house after his wife's death, to manage his servants, and breed her up. And being come to London, to a friend's house, where he lay, in the city, and was joyfully received by him, he did not only take care of his money-affair; but was also resolved to take a little diversion during his stay in London, where he had not been for many years; and accordingly he went to court, and to the play-houses. His friend and he were together one evening at a play, two very handsome, well-dressed, gentlewomen came into the pit, and sat down before them: one of these ladies was very beautiful and genteel, the other seemed to be her companion.

Monsieur du Pont felt a strange alteration in himself at the sight of this woman: he soon got into discourse with her, presented some oranges and sweetmeats to them, and found her conversation as bewitching as her face and mien. His friend kindly cautioned him, but in vain. In fine, the play being done, he prevailed with these ladies to see 'em home, and asked his friend to go along with him, which he unwillingly consented to: so they ushered the ladies to a coach, into which being entered, the ladies bid the coachman drive to a street in Westminster; where, being come, they alighted; and the gentlemen being invited in, came into a very handsome house, genteelly furnished. Here they stayed supper, which was served up by two maid-servants, being cold meat, tarts, and wine. And now entering into a more free conversation, the lady who appeared to be the mistress of the house, being her who was the youngest and most beautiful, told them she was a widow, having buried her husband about two years before, who was a country gentleman, and had left her a moderate fortune, and no child. That finding the country too melancholy for her, she had come to London with this lady, her aunt, who was a widow also; but having had an ill husband, was not so well provided for, as her birth and fortune deserved: That they had taken a house in this part of the town, as most airy and retired, and had but few visitors: and then excused herself with a charming air of modesty, for having admitted these strangers to this freedom, to which indeed Monsieur du Pont had introduced himself with much importunity. In fine, they passed supper in a very agreeable conversation, and then respectfully took leave, after having obtained the two ladies' permission to repeat their visits, and continue the acquaintance chance had so happily begun. One of the maids having called a coach, Monsieur du Pont gave her half a crown, and entered into it with his friend, who pleasantly ridiculed him all the way home, telling him, these ladies were, doubtless kept women and jilts: but Monsieur du Pont was so inflamed with love for the young widow, that he was deaf to all he said, yet seemed to hearken to him, and turn the adventure into a jest, saying, he did not design to visit them any more.

Having come home and gone to bed, the tormenting passion deprived him of rest, and he lay awake all night, thinking on nothing but this charming woman. In short, he visited her the next evening, was entertained with so much modesty and wit that he lost all consideration and resolved, if possible, to gain her for his wife. And now 'tis fit that we should know who she was; and that we relate this fair one's life and adventures, whom we shall call Dorinda, in respect to her family.

CHAPTER 2

She was the younger daughter of a country gentleman of a good family and estate, and though well educated, and very witty and accomplished, yet being wantonly inclined, she at the age of thirteen, fell in love with a young officer of the Guards, who came to the town her father lived in, to visit some relations. This gay young rake, who had a wife and two children in London, made love secretly to this lovely unexperienced girl; and having prevailed with her maid to let him meet her in a grove behind her father's house, there he pretended honorable love to her, and promised to marry her.

In fine, having gained her affections and ruined her, and fearing her father would revenge the injury he had done him, if he came to the knowledge of it; he one evening took leave of her to go for London, pretending that so soon as he had arrived there, he would employ some of his friends to get him a better post, for he was at that time but an ensign; and then he would write down to his relations to move his suit to her father, and get his consent to marry her.

BUT ALAS! the deluded Dorinda, young as she was, too well discerned her lover's base design, and was distracted with shame, love, and revenge. She reproached him, letting fall a shower of tears, in words so tender and so moving, that had he not been a hardened wretch, and one of those heroic rakes that have been versed in every vice this famous city can instruct our youth in, he would have relented; but he was a complete gentleman, had the eloquent tongue of a lawyer, was deceitful as a courtier, had no more religion than honesty, was handsome, lewd, and inconstant; yet he pretended to be much concerned at leaving her, and made a thousand protestations of his fidelity to her. In short, he set out for London the next morning before day, and left the poor undone Dorinda in the utmost despair; yet she did not dare to disclose her grief to any but her treacherous maid, who had been the confident of their amour.

Some months passed without one line from him, by which time she had convincing proofs of her being more unfortunate than she at first imagined, for she found she was with child: this put a thousand dreadful designs into her head, sometimes she resolved to put an end to her wretched life, and prevent her shame; but then reflecting on the miserable state her soul must be in for ever, she desisted from her dismal purpose; and at length, finding it impossible to conceal her misfortune much longer, she resolved to go for London, in search of the base author of her miseries.

In order to this, she got what money she could together, and one evening, having before acquainted her maid with her design, she packed up their clothes, and what rings and other things she had of value; and when all the family were in bed, the maid got two of the men-servants' habits, which they put on, and so disguised, each carrying a bundle, they went away from her father's house by break of day; the maid having ordered her brother, to whom she had told their design, to meet them a little way from the house with horses, on which they mounted, and he being their guide, went with them five and twenty miles, which was near half of the way to London. There they parted from him, paying him well for his trouble, and he took the horses back. Nor did they fear that he would make any discovery, because of being so much concerned in assisting them in their flight.

They lay at the inn that night which he had carried them to, from whence a stage-coach went every other day to London, and was to set out thence the next morning. In this coach they went, and having changed their clothes at a by-alehouse before they came to this inn, and given the men's habits to the fellow with their horses, they appeared to be what they really were; and Dorinda's beauty made a conquest of an old colonel, who, with his son, a youth, was in the coach, and soon entered into discourse with her. She wanted not wit; and her youth, and the fine habit she had on, informed him she was a person of birth. He asked her many questions, and made her large offers of his service.

At last, having been nobly treated by him at dinner, and being now within five miles of London, the unfortunate Dorinda, who knew not where to look for a lodging, nor how to find out the cruel Leander, for so we will call the officer that had undone her, ventured to tell the colonel, that she was a stranger to the town, and should be obliged to him very highly, if he could help her to two things, a lodging in some private house of good reputation, and a sight of Leander, whom she supposed he might have some knowledge of, being an officer. The old gentleman was indeed no stranger to him, nor his vices, and immediately guessed the blushing Dorinda's unhappy condition; he joyfully told her, he was his intimate friend and in his own regiment; that he would carry her to a lady's house who was his relation, and should serve her in all things she could desire. Dorinda looked on this as a providence: But, alas, it was a prelude to greater misfortunes and her entire ruin. For this colonel, now believing her already ruined, had his own satisfaction in view, and pitying her condition, knowing his friend was already married, thought it would be a deed of charity in him to take care of and keep her himself.

In order to which, so soon as the coach came to the inn in Holborn, he had a hackney called, into which he sent his son and a servant that he had with him, who rode up one of his horses, home to his own house, and went with the lady and her maid to a house at Westminster, where a useful lady lived, that is in plain English a private quality-bawd, who used to lodge a mistress for him at any time; a woman who was well bred, and a very saint in appearance, and lived so privately that her neighbors knew nothing of her profession; she passed for a widow-gentlewoman who let lodgings to people of fashion; she kept a maid-servant, and had always one handsome young woman or other a boarder with her, who she pretended were her kinswomen out of the country, being called aunt by one, and cousin by another, as she directed the poor creatures to style her. The house was neatly furnished, and had no person in it at that time but the ruined Miranda, who afterwards went with Dorinda, and was with her at the play, when Monsieur du Pont met with them.

The colonel presented Dorinda to this good lady, giving her a great charge to be careful of and kind to her: And indeed the procuress, Mrs. seeing her so young and handsome, and so well rigged, was mighty glad of her company, and resolved to use all her devilish arts to gain her esteem and friendship, in hopes to make a good penny of her. Some wine and a supper were soon got, and the colonel pressing Dorinda to know who she was and her circumstances, got her to own to him that his friend had promised her marriage, and ruined her; but she would not tell him her true name, nor from whence she came, but with tears besought him to bring Leander to her, which he promised to do the next morning: so took leave, much charmed with Dorinda, and in his own thoughts condemning his friend's baseness.

He went to his own home to his wife and family, and the poor distracted Dorinda was conducted with her maid to a handsome chamber; where, the door being locked, and she and her servant being laid in bed, she began to reflect on her own condition and actions. It is impossible to describe in words what she felt when she considered, that she had left her tender parents, blasted the reputable family she belonged to, since none but must guess the cause of her sudden flight; that she was now in a strange place, and in the hands of those she knew nothing of; that in case Leander, from whom she had little cause to expect any good, refused to marry and take care of her, she was ruined to all intents and purposes; could no more return to her home and family, nor had with her half enough to provide long for her and the helpless infant she was likely to bring into the world. She shed a flood of tears, and wished for death a thousand times, and passed the night without closing her eyes.

Thus by one imprudent action we often ruin the peace and quiet of our lives forever, and by one false step undo ourselves. I wish mankind would but reflect how barbarous a deed it is, how much below a man, nay how like the devil it is, to debauch a young unexperienced virgin, and expose to ruin and an endless train of miseries, the person whom his persuasions has drawn to gratify his desire, and to oblige him at the expense of her own peace and honor. And surely if our laws be just, that punishes that man with death who kills another, he certainly merits that or something worse, that is, eternal infamy, who betrays the foolish maid that credits his oaths and vows, and abandons her to shame and misery. And if women were not infatuated, doubtless every maid would look on the man that proposes such a question to her, as her mortal enemy, and from that moment banish him from her heart and company.

FORGIVE THIS DIGRESSION. Dorinda's condition and wrongs must inspire every generous mind with some concern and resentment against mankind.

The colonel, who dreamed of her all night, and was on fire to possess her, sent for his friend Leander in the morning to a tavern, told him of his adventure, and asked him what he meant to do with her, and who she was: But to this last question he was dumb, well knowing that the wretched Dorinda was the colonel's own niece, being his sister's daughter. He said she was a country squire's daughter in another town, and that he could do nothing for her, but give her a piece of money, and remove her to a cheap lodging, and send her back to her father's when she was up again. But the colonel reproved him, and said he would himself pay her lodging, and contribute something towards providing for her: nay, in short, that if he would quit her company, he would keep her. But Leander was startled at this proposal, fearing he would discover who she was, and that it would be a quarrel between them, and his ruin. He desired some time to consider of that; and concluded to go immediately with him to see her.

They found her up, her eyes swollen with weeping: At the moment Leander entered the chamber, she swooned; his love revived, he caught her in his arms; and the colonel, disordered with this sight, went downstairs, and left them alone with none but the maid, who shutting the door, left them together. It is needless to relate what passionate expressions passed on her side, and excuses on his. In fine, he told her she was in an ill house, that the colonel had bad designs upon her, and that he would that evening fetch her away and take care of her; that she should not discover who she was, as she valued her own peace and his life. In fine, poor Dorinda, born to be deceived, gave credit to all he said, and followed his directions. The colonel and he went away together; and in the evening Leander, having gone to an obscure midwife's at St. Giles's, and took a lodging for her, fetched her away and carried her thither, pretending great fondness.

Here she continued some time, never stirring out of doors. He continually visited her, and told the colonel he had sent her into the country. At last she was delivered of a dead child, and lay long ill of a fever. And now Leander being quite tired with the expense, proposed to her to return home. She urged his promises and vows to marry her, till he was obliged to disclose the fatal secret to her, that he was married already. But what words can express her resentments and disorder at that instant? In short, he left her in this distraction, and that evening sent her a letter to call him in a coach alone at a tavern he appointed, saying he had thought of a means to make her easy.

She imprudently went, and there he had hired two bailiffs to arrest her with a sham action. She was by them carried to a sponging-house, and there kept whilst he sold his post, and with his family went into the country; having the night he trepanned her, took away from the midwife's her clothes, money and jewels, and discharged the maid; who not daring to return to her friends or mistress's father's, went down to an aunt she had in another shire: And when Leander had dispatched his business and was gone, the officers told her he had released her, and she might go where she pleased.

She was so weak she could scarce walk, nor knew one step of the way, or the name of the place she was in. One of these fellows was so moved with her complaints, that he led her to the midwife's house as she directed, having learned the name of the street during her abode with her. The midwife, who knew nothing of what she had suffered, received her with amazement, and soon gave her an account how Leander had taken away all her clothes, and sent away her maid, which so afflicted Dorinda that she went half dead to bed; and in the morning, not knowing what other course to take, having neither clothes nor money, and the midwife being poor, giving her to understand she could not long entertain her, she resolved to seek out the generous colonel.

In order to which she desired the midwife to go with her in a coach to the lady's house at Westminster, to which he had at first carried her: They went, found the house, and were received by Mrs. with much civility and kindness; the colonel was sent for, and came before dinner: he took her in his arms with transport, protested never to part with, but take care of her to death. She related to him Leander's base usage of her. He told her he had sold his post, and left the town: And in short, the midwife being treated and rewarded for bringing her thither, took leave. The best rooms in the house were ordered for Dorinda, and the colonel did that night sleep in her arms: Thus her first misfortune involved her in a worse.

Some months she lived in this manner, being richly clothed and bravely maintained by her old gallant, who doted upon her. In this time she contracted a great friendship with a young woman in the house, Miranda, who was very handsome, good-natured, and about the age of twenty: They were continually together, and lay in one bed when the colonel did not come to lie there. By this means they became so intimate, that Miranda gave her an account who she was, and how she came there.

CHAPTER 3

Miranda told Dorinda she was the daughter of an eminent divine, who had seven children, and very good preferments in the country; but living very high, and breeding his children up at a great rate, provided no fortunes for them, so that dying before they were placed out in the world, they were left to shift, and she being one of the youngest, being then about thirteen, was taken by a lady to wait on a little daughter she had about seven years old, and with the family brought up to town. that in a year's time her master, who was a young gentleman, ruined her; and fearing her lady should discover the intrigue, persuaded her to quit her service, pretending sickness, and that London did not agree with her; and take leave of her lady to return to her mother, who kept a boarding-school in the country to maintain herself and the children, two of the boys being yet at school, and two girls at home.

But she went not to her mother as she pretended, but into a lodging her master had provided for her. In this house, he for two years maintained and kept her company; but at last growing weary, gave her a small allowance, so that by the bawd's persuasions, she admitted others to her embraces, and was at this time maintained by a merchant in the city, and concluded her story with many tears; saying, she did not like this course of life, and wished she could find a way to leave it; but that the bawd always kept her bare of money by borrowing and wheedling it out of her, and that they were always poor and wanting money, living, as she saw, very high in diet; that she had had several children, but had but one alive, and that was at nurse at Chelsey, being a little girl, about three years old, which she had by a young lord, who took care of it.

Dorinda promised to serve her in all she was able. And now a strange turn happened in her affairs: for the colonel's brother-in-law, Dorinda's father, having made all the inquiry after his daughter that was possible in the country, and offered a reward to any that should inform him what was become of her, was at last acquainted with the manner of her going to London by the maid's brother who had procured the horses for them; on which news he came away for London in search of her; he arrived at his brother, the colonel's house, tells him his business, and begs his assistance to find her out, knowing nothing who had debauched her at first, nor why she fled; though he too rightly guessed that must be the occasion of her withdrawing herself.

The colonel, who had never seen his niece Dorinda in the country, having not been at his brother's house for many years past, was a little surprised at the circumstances of time and place where he met with this young woman, and longed to get to her to question her about it. It was night when his brother arrived, so he was obliged to delay satisfying his curiosity till the morning; then he went to Dorinda, and telling her the reason of his coming, and that her father was come, she swooned, and by that too well convinced him, that he had lain with his own niece, and not only committed a great sin, but dishonoured his family.

He at this moment felt the stings of guilt, and bitter repentance; he resolved never more to commit the like. And now of an amorous lover, who used to teach her vice, he became a wise monitor, and preached up virtue and repentance; and told her, he would that day remove her from that ill house, and place her in the country, give her a maintenance to live honestly, and, if possible, dispose of her to advantage; that he would endeavour to reconcile her to her father, provided she would never disclose what had passed between them. She gladly agreed to all: and here providence was so merciful as to give her an opportunity of being happy again; but, alas, youth once vitiated is rarely reformed, and woman, who whilst virtuous is an angel, ruined and abandoned by the man she loves, becomes a devil. The bawd had prevented all these good designs from coming to effect, by introducing a young nobleman into her company, the most gay agreeable man in the world, who was very liberal to the procuress, and made Dorinda such large presents, and used such rhetoric, that she could not resist his solicitations, but yielded to his desires.

She was for this cause deaf to reason, and acquainted Miranda and Mrs. what had passed between her uncle and her: so it was agreed that she should go where her uncle desired, get what she could, and return to them. In the evening the colonel came and took her, and her clothes away, and carried her to Chelsey to a widow gentlewoman's house that was his friend. The next morning he returned with her father, having told him, that Leander had ruined her; and that having fled to London, she had found a lady of his acquaintance out, where she had been taken care of for four days past, having been abandoned and ill used by Leander: that he had heard of it from this lady but the day before his arrival, and counseled him to forgive her, and take her home again, or continue her with this good lady to live privately, and allow her something. This was what the colonel had contrived, and taught Dorinda to say.

The father heard this with great grief, and swore to take revenge upon Leander; but that heaven prevented, for they had news of his death soon after, being thrown from off his horse as he was hunting, and killed on the spot, in which heaven's justice was sadly manifested. Now doting upon the unfortunate Dorinda, he consented to see and provide for her, but not to carry her home to his wife and other daughters, lest it should publish his misfortune more: but resolved to allow her a convenient maintenance to live with this gentlewoman, and at his return to say, that she was run away with, and married to a person much below what he expected, belonging to the sea; and that he had done what he thought fit for her, and left her in town. This, he thought, would silence his neighbours and afflicted wife, who had been long indisposed with the grief she had fallen into on her account.

'Tis needless to relate what passed between the father and daughter at their first meeting; the disorder both were in was extraordinary: but having promised to allow her thirty pounds a year, on condition she lived soberly and retired in this gentlewoman's house, and dispatched some other affairs that he had to do in town, he returned home; and she remained some days in this place, her uncle visiting, and frequently admonishing her to live well and repent of her follies. But she could not bear this confinement, but longed to see her young lover and friend Miranda again: in short, she watched her opportunity one morning, when the gentlewoman went out to a friend that lay sick, who had sent for her; and packed up her clothes, called a boat, and left a letter on the table for her uncle, to tell him, she was gone to town to live, to the house where he had placed her in before, where she should be glad to see him; and so went away to Mrs. where she was joyfully received.

The colonel soon received the news of her flight, and the letter, and went to her, and used all arguments to persuade her thence, but to no purpose; so she continued there, and had variety of lovers; learning all the base arts of that vile profession: till at last, having been so cunning as to have laid up a thousand pounds, besides a great stock of rich clothes, a watch, necklace, rings, and some plate, having lived in several lodgings, and been kept by several men of fashion, she took Miranda, and furnished a house, kept two maid-servants, and Miranda's pretty girl, and lived genteelly, being visited by none but such lovers as could pay well for their entertainment.

THESE WERE Dorinda's adventures past, and the circumstance in which Monsieur du Pont found her; he visited her every day, and could not think of leaving London without Dorinda. She wisely considering with herself how precarious the way of life she followed was, resolved to marry him, but cunningly delayed it in order to increase his passion; pretending that she could not marry so soon after the death of her first husband, being but two years a widow. Monsieur du Pont confessed his design of marrying her to his friend; and though he was much averse to it, yet having no particular knowledge of her, he could not allege anything to deter him from it but his own conjectures. In fine, Monsieur du Pont in two months time got her consent, and taking his friend along with him, one fatal morning went to her house, from whence she, accompanied with her friend and confidant Miranda, went with them to St. Martin's Church, where the knot was tied, and the unfortunate du Pont sealed his ruin.

They returned to her house, where they dined merrily, and Monsieur du Pont lay that night. In a few days after their marriage, he importuned her to go home with him into the country, which she was no ways averse to, because she feared the visits of her customers, some of whom could not be well denied admittance by reason of their quality, and power over her; which would discover all to him. He was much pleased at her appearing so ready to comply with his desires; and now they prepared for going. At her request, he consented to give Miranda the best part of the furniture in the house, which she designed to continue in, and follow the unhappy trade she had so long been versed in, though in reality she was much averse to it, and wished from the bottom of her soul, that she could meet with some honest man that would marry her, to whom she would be true and virtuous, being no ways addicted to vice, but reduced to it by misfortune and necessity.

And now Dorinda thought to go privately to her uncle the colonel, to acquaint him with her good fortune, in hopes he would now appear to credit her. She pretended to him great repentance for her past follies, and he gladly received her, visited her husband, and owned her for his niece; sent down word to her parents, who were overjoyed to hear she was reclaimed, and so well disposed of. Her mother came to town to see her long lost child. And now, had she had the least spark of virtue, she had been truly happy. Monsieur du Pont at last carried her home in the stage-coach, having sent her clothes, plate, and what else they thought fit by the wagon, and returned five hundred pounds, which she had called in from the goldsmith's where she had placed it, by bills to Bristol.

They arrived safe, and she was welcomed by all his friends, and treated handsomely. She pretended to be charmed with Charlotta his beautiful daughter. And for some months they lived very happily.

CHAPTER 4

But, alas, a virtuous life and the quiet country were things that did not relish well with a woman who had lived a town-life. Dorinda wanted pleasure, and soon fixed her wanton eyes upon a young sea-captain who used to visit at Monsieur du Pont's. This young gentleman had been exchanged with a merchant's son in France who was related to Monsieur du Pont, and so became intimate with him, and many French captains of ships and merchants. He was very handsome and loved his pleasures, being a true friend to a handsome woman and a bottle. Dorinda soon made herself understood by him, and he as soon answered her desires, and made Monsieur du Pont the fashionable thing, a cuckold. She grew big with child, and was delivered of a daughter, which Monsieur du Pont, who had discovered something of her intrigue with the young captain, Mr. Farley, did not look on with the same tenderness as he did on Charlotta; for which reason she now beheld her with much indignation and dislike, though she concealed her malice and seemed fond of her.

Charlotta did all she was able to please her; but now having a child of her own, Dorinda wished her out of the world; and her little darling Diana growing every day more lovely in her eyes, and her husband seeming more reserved to her, and to take little notice of the child, so enraged her, that she resolved to get Charlotta out of her way if possible, that Diana might inherit all the fortune. Captain Farley went a voyage or two to France and Holland, and returning, when he came back to visit her, she made known her wicked design to him, and in fine, gained him to assist her in it.

They contrived to send her beyond sea by some captain of his acquaintance, and he pitched upon a French master of a ship, who was used to trade to Virginia and the Leeward-Islands, a man who was of a cruel avaricious disposition, and would do any thing for money; his name was Monsieur la Roque. Farley expected him hourly in that port. Mrs. du Pont, and her husband, and Charlotta had often gone together on board ships to be treated by merchants and masters of her husband's acquaintance, and sometimes without her husband with some other friends, and particularly Farley. Captain la Roque being arrived at Bristol with his ship, which was bound to Virginia, Farley acquainted him with their design on Charlotta, and offered him such a bribe as easily prevailed with the covetous Frenchman to undertake to effect it.

So soon as he was ready to sail, he gave them notice; and now the fatal day was come when the innocent lovely virgin, who was in the thirteenth year of her age, was to be deprived of her dear father and friends, and exposed to all the dangers of the seas, and more cruel relentless men. Monsieur du Pont going to take a walk with a neighboring gentleman, Captain Farley came with the French captain to invite Mrs. du Pont and Charlotta on board; she in obedience to her mother-in-law's desires went with her in the captain's boat, and being come on board they were highly treated, and something being put into some wine that was given Charlotta, she was so bereft of her senses, that they put her on the captain's bed, and left her senseless, whilst they took leave of him and went on shore in a chance-boat which they called passing by the ship, which weighed anchor and set sail immediately.

And now Mrs. du Pont, as they had contrived, so soon as they were on shore, began to wring her hands and cry like one distracted, pretending Charlotta was drowned: She alarmed all the people as she went along, saying, that she fell over the side of the boat into the sea, and no help being near, was drowned: None could contradict her, because no body could tell what boat they came in from the ship, the boat being gone off before she made the outcry. Being come home, she threw herself upon her bed; and her husband being informed of this sad news by the laments of the servants at his entering into his house, and going up to her, asking a hundred questions of the manner of it; she so rarely acted her part, that he believed she was really grieved, and Charlotta certainly drowned; which so struck him to the heart, that he was seized with a deep melancholy, and spent most part of his days in his closet shut up from company, and the mornings and evenings walking alone in some retired place, or by the sea-shore; so that Dorinda flattered herself that she should soon be a widow, and return to her dear London.

And here it is necessary that we leave them, to inquire after the innocent Charlotta, who waking about midnight, was quite amazed to find herself on a bed no bigger than a couch, shut up in a closet, and hearing the seamen's voices, soon discovered the fatal secret, and knew that she was in the ship: she knocked loudly at the cabin-door, upon which a young gentleman opened it, a youth of excellent shape and features, in a fine habit; he had a candle in his hand, and seemed to view her with admiration.

"Lovely maid," said he, "what would you please to have?"

"I beg to know, Sir," said she, "where my mother and Captain Farley are, and why I am left here alone?"

He remained silent a moment, and then bowing, answered, "Madam, I am sorry that I must be so unfortunate as to acquaint you with ill news the first time that I have the honor to speak to you: They are gone ashore, and have sold you to the captain. I am a passenger in this ship, and shall, I hope, be the instrument of your deliverance out of his cruel hands. I was onshore when you were left here, but having seen you come on board, I made haste back, and finding the ship just under sail, upon my entrance into it asked him where you were; on which he told me with joy, that he had you safe in his cabin, having received a good sum to carry you with us to Virginia. I love you,

Charlotta, with the greatest sincerity, and will lose my life in your defense, both to secure your virtue and your liberty. This is not the first time I have seen you."

At these words he sat down by her, pressed her hand, and kissed her. But what words can express her confusion and grief! She fetched a great sigh and fainted, at which the young gentleman ran and fetched some cordial-water from his chest, and gave her; at which reviving, she fell into a transport of sorrow, calling on Heaven to help and deliver her. He waited till her passion was a little mitigated, and then began to reason with and comfort her, telling her, she must submit to the Almighty's will, and that she should look upon his being in that ship as an earnest of God's favor to and care of her: 'That he was in circumstances that rendered him capable of serving her; that his name was Belanger, and that his father and hers had been intimate friends, being a merchant who lived at St. Malos, but was dead about seven months before, having left him and one daughter in guardians' hands, he not being yet of age: That these guardians used him and his sister ill, having put her into a monastery against her will, being engaged to a young gentleman whom they would not let her marry, pretending that he was not a suitable match in fortune, and that she was too young, being but fourteen, to dispose of herself; which they did with no other design, as he supposed, but to keep her fortune in their hands as long as they could, in hopes that both he and she might die single, and leave all in their power, being his uncles by his father's side, and heirs to the fortune which was very considerable, in case they died without issue. That old Monsieur Belanger having effects to a great value in Virginia in the hands of a gentleman who was brother to Madam Belanger his deceased mother, he was going to this uncle to get them, and to ask his assistance to deal with his guardians, whom he had left, because he had some reason to fear that they designed to poison him; having been informed by a trusty servant who had lived with his father long, and was now left in his house at St. Malos, that he had overheard them contriving his death; that he had taken with him a good sum of money, and some merchandize to trade with in Virginia."

And thus Monsieur Belanger having acquainted Charlotta with his circumstances, concluded with many promises to take care of her in the voyage, get her out of the captain's hands, and marry her when he came to Virginia. She heard him attentively, and answered with great modesty, that if he did protect her from being injured by others, and acted in delivering her as he pretended, both she and her father, if they lived to meet again, would endeavor to be grateful to him: That she had now resigned herself to God, and was resolved to submit to what he pleased to permit her to suffer, and to prefer death to dishonor. He embraced her knees, and vowed to preserve her virtue, and never suffer her to be wronged or taken from him whilst he had a drop of blood left in his veins, but to merit her favor by all that man could do, which he as nobly performed as freely promised.

And now poor Charlotta had none but him to comfort her; and though she strove all she was able, yet grief so weakened her, that in few days she was confined to her bed. It is needless to relate all that the tender lover did to render himself dear to the mistress of his heart; he tended and watched with her many nights, sat on her bedside, and told the tedious hours, alarmed with every change of her distemper, which was an intermitting fever: he feed the surgeon largely to save her, and at last had the satisfaction to see her recovering; youth and medicines both uniting, restored the charming maid to health, and Belanger to his repose of mind who now seeing the ship not many leagues from the desired port, flattered himself that she should be his. But, alas, fate had otherwise determined; their faith and virtue was to meet with greater trials yet and the time was far off before they should be happy.

CHAPTER 5

A pirate-ship came up with them in forty five degrees of latitude, bearing English colors, which seemed to be no merchant-ship, but a frigate with thirty guns, well manned, and they soon discovered who they were by their firing at them and putting up a bloody flag, bidding them surrender with their dreadful cannon. The French Captain la Roque did on this occasion all that a brave man could, nor did Monsieur Belanger fail to show his courage, but fought both for his mistress and liberty till he was wounded in many places, and retiring into the cabin to have his wounds dressed, found the affrighted Charlotta lying in a swoon on the floor.

At this sight he forgot himself, and catching her up in his arms fell back with her, and having lost much blood, fainted; mean time the villain la Roque was killed on the deck, and the enemies entering the ship, soon mastered the few that were left to oppose them, and coming into the cabin, saw the fair Charlotta and her lover holding her clasped in his arms as if resolved in death not to part with her. The pirates, for such they were who had taken the ship, being English, French and Irish men belonging to the crew at Madagascar, were moved at this sight; particularly a desperate young man that commanded the pirate-ship, he was charmed with the face of the reviving Charlotta, who lifting up her bright eyes ravished his soul; he raised her up in his arms, forcing Belanger's hands to let her go, he being still senseless.

She looked upon him with much amazement, but was silent with fear. The pirate-captain comforted her with tender words, then she fell at his feet, and intreated him to pity her companion, that gentleman. He presently ordered some wine to be given him, had him laid on a bed, and his wounds dressed; then left her with him, whilst he gave orders how to dispose of the goods and men that were left alive in the ship, commanding the richest merchandize, some provisions, and the guns, and powder in it, to be carried aboard his own ship, and the men and merchant-ship to be dismissed with what he thought sufficient to support them till they reached Barbados or Virginia, excepting no person but the fair virgin and her lover.

Whilst he saw these things done, and searched the ship, Charlotta had time to bewail her sad state and her lover's, who was now so overwhelmed with grief and pain that he could scarce utter his thoughts in these moving expressions: "My dear Charlotta, it is our hard fate to be now left here alone in the hands of men whose obdurate hearts are insensible to pity, from whom we can expect nothing but ill usage, did not your angelic face too well convince me that they will spare your life. Oh! could I find a way to secure your virtue, though with the loss of my life, I should die with pleasure: but, alas, you must be sacrificed, and I be left the most unhappy wretch on Earth, if Providence does not prevent it by some miracle or by death. Say, my angel, what can we do?"

Charlotta shedding a flood of tears, replied, "My dear preserver, my only hope on Earth, all a weak virgin can do to preserve her honor, I will do, and only death shall part us; but let me caution you to say you are my brother, for the pirate captain seems to look on me with some concern; I fear affection: and if so, should he discover ours to one another, it might ruin us, and cause the villain to destroy you to possess me, who being left in his hands when you are gone, shall be forced to what my soul abhors more than death."

Belanger pressing her hand, replied, "Alas, there needed only that dreadful thought to end me;" and so fainted: her shrieks brought the pirate-captain, who was an Irish gentleman (whose story we shall relate hereafter) down to the cabin-door, who seeing her wringing her hands over the pale young man who lay senseless, began to suspect he was her lover, and was fired with jealousy: however he ran to her, and lifting her up in his arms, asked her, who this person was for whom she was so greatly concerned? She answered, he was her brother, that they were going from France to Virginia to a rich uncle, having been cheated by their guardians of their fortune in France. And then she fell on her knees, and besought him with tears to land them on that coast, or put them into the next ship he met with bound to that place or near it.

Appeased with hearing he was her brother, though doubtful of the truth, he embraced her, and promised to do what she desired; commanding his surgeon and crew to do all that was necessary to save the young man's life and recover him. Cordials being given him, and his wounds carefully dressed, he got strength daily. Mean time the captain had them carefully watched to discover whether he was her brother or not, resolving to get rid of him if his rival: but Charlotta being on her guard, so well behaved herself, that he could get no satisfaction for some time.

He daily importuned her with his passion for her in Belanger's presence, on whom she was continually attending; and told her, if she would consent to marry him when they came a-shore at the Island of Providence, which was at that time the pirates' place of rendezvous, he would make her the richest lady in Christendom, and give her brother a fortune, having such immense treasures buried there in the earth of jewels and gold, as would purchase them a retreat, and all things else they could desire in this world. To all these offers she gave little answer, but modestly excused herself from making any promises, saying she was too young to marry yet, and would consider farther of it when they came a-shore, yet thanked him for his generous treatment of them.

These delays still more inflamed him; he grew every day more earnest and importunate, and often proceeded to kiss her in

Belanger's presence, whose inward grief can hardly be described, which his face often betrayed by turning pale, whilst his enraged soul sparkled in his fiery eyes when he saw his mistress rudely folded in another's arms. One day Charlotta, willing to change the discourse of love, begged the pirate-captain to inform her who he was, and how he came to follow this unhappy course of life; "perhaps," said she, "being convinced you are well descended, as your gentleman-like treatment of us inclines me to believe, I shall esteem you more." Glad to oblige her, he began the story of his life in this manner.

CHAPTER 6

I was born in Ireland, divine Charlotta, of a noble and loyal family, who fighting for King James II were undone: my father fell with honour in the field, our estate was afterwards confiscated, and my poor mother, a lord's daughter, left with three helpless children, of whom I was the eldest, exposed to want. I was then eighteen, and had a soul that could not bear misfortunes, or endure to see my mother's condition; so I took my young sister, who was but ten years old, and fair as an angel, and leaving my mother, and my brother, but an infant, at a relation's house, who charitably took them in, escaped from my ruined country and friends to France, hoping to get some honourable post there, under that hospitable generous king who had received my prince. When we arrived at St. Germans, having spent what little our kind friends had given us at our first setting out from home, we were received but coldly. My sister, indeed, was by a French lady taken to be a companion for her eldest daughter, something so like a servant, that my soul burned with indignation. I waited long to get preferment, living on charity, that is, eating at others' tables. At last I fell in company with some desperate young gentlemen, who, like me, were tired with this uncertain course of life, some of whom had been bred to the sea: we agreed to go separately to Brest, and seize in the night some small vessel ready victualled, and equipped for a voyage, some of us having first gone aboard as passengers. This design we executed with so good success, that finding a small merchant-ship bound for Martinico, we sent five of our companions, being in all fourteen, as passengers, on board with our trunks of clothes; and pretending to take leave of them, all followed, staying till night drinking healths with the French captain, who suspected nothing, and had but eight hands aboard of twenty-six that belonged to the ship, which was designed to weigh anchor, and set sail the next day. We seized upon him first, and then on his men, singing so loud that they were not heard to dispute by the ships who were lying near us in the harbour: we bound and put them all under hatches, and set sail immediately, resolving to make for the island of Jamaica, where we hoped to sell the merchandize we had in the ship, which was laden with rich goods; and having made our fortunes there, to go for Holland, and settle ourselves as merchants, or look out for some other way to make ourselves easy, and gain some settlement in the world.

When we were got to sea, we fetched the captain up, and told him partly our design: he begged to be set ashore with his men, at some port of France; pleading he had a wife and seven children, and was undone if we carried him thence in that manner. So we consented to his desire, and at break of day gave him one of the boats, and six of the men to carry him to land, which I suppose he got safely to, having heard nothing more of him. And now we put out all the sail we could, and had a prosperous voyage, till we came near Jamaica: there we met a pirate-sloop well-manned and armed, carrying French colours: we were now most of us sick, and in great want of fresh water and provisions. They gave us a signal to lie by, and we supposing them to be friends, obeyed, joyful to meet a ship to assist us: but they soon made us sensible of our mistake, sending their boat's crew on board, who seized us and our ship, and carried us all fettered to the island of Providence; where, in short, we grew intimate with these and other pirates, and consented to pursue the same course of life. They did not trust us in one ship together, but dividing us, took us out with them.

Ten of us have already lost our lives bravely; three are married, and command ships like me; we have vast treasures, and live like princes on the spoils of others. It is true, it is no safe employment, for we are continually in danger of death: hanging or drowning are what we are to expect; but we are so daring and hardened by custom, that we regard it as nothing. For my own part, I am often stung with remorse, and on reflection wish to quit this course of life: I am ashamed to think of the brutish actions I have done, and the innocent blood I have spilt, makes me uneasy, and apprehensive of death.

And now, sweet Charlotta, I have told you my unhappy story, it is in your power to reclaim and make me happy: promise then to be mine, and I will marry you, and take all the treasure I am master of, and with your brother sail for Virginia; from thence we'll go for Ireland as passengers. You shall acquaint your uncle that we have been taken by pirates, and left on that place; for my ship shall in the night make off, and the boat having landed us, shall return to it; so that we and our wealth shall be left without fear of discovery. Then he addressed himself to Belanger, saying, Sir, I have treated you, for your sister's sake, kindly and generously; I expect you should lay your commands upon her to consent to my request: I would not be obliged to use the methods I can take to procure what I now sue for; but if I am constrained to use force, it will be your own faults. At these words he went out of the cabin much disordered, and left them in great perplexity; a death-like paleness overspread their faces, and they sat silent for some moments.

Then Belanger fetching a deep sigh, casting his eyes up to heaven, said, "Now, my God, manifest thy goodness to us, and deliver us." Charlotta would have spoken, the tears streaming down her pale cheeks, but he stopped her from declaring her sad thoughts, saying softly, "Hush my angel, we are watched, betray not the fatal secret that will bring death to me, and ruin you." They composed their looks as much as possible; and three days passed, in which the pirate-captain grew so importunate with Charlotta, that she was forced to declare herself in some manner, and told him she was engaged to a gentleman in France.

At last he grew enraged, and told her, he was too well acquainted with the reason of her coldness towards him; and since fair means would not do, he would try other methods. At these words he called for some of the crew, who seizing on Belanger, put him in irons, and carried him down into the hold. Charlotta, transported with grief at this dismal sight, threw herself at the pirate's feet, and told him, "'Tis in vain, cruel man, that you endeavour to force me to consent to your desires, I have a soul that scorns to yield to threats; nay, death shall not fright me into a compliance with your unjust request: I have already given my heart and faith to another, and am now resolved never to eat or drink again, till you release my husband, for such he is by plighted vows and promises, which I will never break: no, I will be equally deaf to prayers and threats; and if you use force, death shall free me. This is my last resolve, do as you please." At these words she rose and left him, and sat down with a look so resolute and calm, that his soul shook: he sat down by her, and reasoned with her: "Charlotta," said he, "why do you force me to be cruel? I love you passionately, and cannot live without you: Heaven will absolve you from the vows you have made, since you shall break them by necessity, not choice; that sin I shall be answerable for: my passion makes me as deaf to reason, as you are to pity: I beg you would consider ere it is too late, and I am drove to use the last extremity to gain you. Your lover's life is in my power: be kind, and he may live, and be happy with some other maid; if you refuse my offers, he shall surely die; I give you to this night to resolve." At these words he left her, setting a watch at the cabin-door, and taking everything from her that could harm her. Then he went to the quarter-deck, and calling for Belanger, who was brought up to him loaded with irons, he used threats, entreaties, and all he could think of, to make him consent to part with Charlotta, and assist him to gain her; all which he rejected with scorn and disdain. At last he was so enraged, that he caused Belanger to be stripped, and lashed in a cruel manner, who bravely stifled his groans, and would not once complain, lest Charlotta should hear him, and be driven to despair.

But the pirate's rage did not end here; he had him carried down and shown to her, the blood running down his tender back and arms, and gagged, that he might not speak to her; but she, doubtless, inspired with courage from above, supported this dreadful sight with great constancy and calmness. "'Tis the will of Heaven," said she, "my dear Belanger, that we should suffer thus: be constant, as I will be, God will deliver us by death or miracle."

The pirate ordered him back to the hold, some brandy being given him to drink, which he refused. And now he resolved to gratify his flame, by enjoying Charlotta at midnight by force: in order to which he left her under a guard, and returned not to her till the dead of night, when, being laid on the bed in her cabin weeping and praying, almost spent with extreme grief and abstinence, he stole gently to her, having put on Belanger's coat, in hopes to deceive her the more easily; then laying his cheek to hers, he whispered, "Charming Charlotta, see your glad lover loosened from his chains, flies to your arms." She, as one awakened from a horrid dream, trembling, and in suspense, lifted up her eyes amazed, and thought him to be Belanger; when he, impatient to accomplish his base design, proceeding to further freedoms beyond modesty, discovered to her the deceit, which she, inspired by her good angel, seemed not to know; but taking a sharp bodkin out of her hair, stabbed him in the belly so dangerously, that he fell senseless on the bed.

At this instant a sailor cried out, "A sail, a sail; where's our captain?" This alarmed all the crew, and the gunner running to the great cabin-door, which the captain had locked when he went in, knocked and called; but only Charlotta answered, he was coming. Meantime the ship they had seen coming up, gave them such a broadside, as made the whole crew run to their arms: a bloody fight ensued, and Charlotta consulting what to do, believing the pirate-captain dead, and being well assured the ship that fought with that she was in, must be some man of war or frigate come in pursuit of the pirates, because she first attacked them, resolved to disguise herself, and go out of the cabin to see the event, hoping the danger they were in would make them free Belanger.

She caught up a cloak that lay in the cabin, and a hat, and so disguised opened the door; but seeing a horrid sight between the ship's crew and the Spaniards, who had now boarded her, (for it was a Spanish man of war, who was sent out to scour the pirates in those parts, and having met the French ship out of which Charlotta had been taken, and by them got intelligence of this pirate-ship, was come in pursuit of them) she did not dare to venture farther than the door. Meantime the pirate-captain recovering from his swoon, got up, so wounded and faint with loss of blood, that he could scarce crawl to the door, from which he pushed Charlotta, whom he did not at that instant know: he called for help, but seeing the enemy driving his men back upon him, sword in hand, he endeavoured to take down a cutlass that was near him, and fell down. And now the Spaniards having mastered the pirates, who were almost all killed or grievously wounded, gave over the slaughter; and having secured those that were alive, the Spanish captain, who was not only a brave, but a most accomplished young gentleman, with some of his officers, entered the great cabin, in which Charlotta and the half-dead pirate were: she immediately cast off her disguise, and threw herself at his feet, begging him in the French tongue, to pity and protect her, and a young gentleman whom the pirate had put in irons, in the hold, whose life she valued above her own.

He gazed upon her with admiration; her beauty and youth were such advocates, as a gallant Spaniard could not refuse anything to: he took her up in his arms, promised her all she desired, and commanded the young gentleman should be immediately looked for, and, if living, set at liberty. Belanger had heard the guns and noise, and none but a brave man can be sensible of what he felt whilst he lay bound in chains, whilst his mistress's distress and liberty were disputed, he was even ready to tear his limbs off to get free from his fetters; but Heaven preserved his life by keeping him thus confined, who else had been exposed to all the dangers of the fight. The Spaniards soon found and freed him, bringing him up to the cabin, where Charlotta received him with transport; and Gonzalo the Spanish captain, and his friends, gave him joy of his freedom. The pirate-captain, at her entreaty, was taken care of by the surgeon, his wound dressed, and he put to bed, being almost senseless, and in great danger of death. And now a sufficient number of men, with a lieutenant, being left on board the pirate-ship, Belanger and Charlotta having all that belonged to them restored by the brave Spaniard, went on board his ship, where they were highly treated, and might in safety bless God, and enjoy some repose. The Spanish ship was bound for the island of St. Domingo, from whence our lovers hoped to get passage to Virginia, little fore-seeing what changes of fortune they were to meet with in the island they were going to. There was on board the Spanish ship a young gentleman named Don Antonio de Medenta, the son of the Governor of St. Domingo, who went, attended by two servants, as a volunteer, to show his courage, and for pleasure.

He was very handsome, and of a daring and impatient temper, ambitious and resolute, much respected by all that knew him, his father's darling, and, in short, a man who could bear no contradiction. He was so charmed with Charlotta, that he was uneasy out of her sight; and though he at first checked his passion, as knowing she was promised to Belanger, yet it daily increasing, he began to hate him as his rival, and meditate how to take her from him. It is the nature of the Spaniards, we all know, to be close and very subtle in their designs, very amorous, and very revengeful: this cavalier wisely concealed his passion from her, and contrived to get his ends so well, that he effected it without appearing criminal.

In their passage to St. Domingo, they met a small French merchant-ship bound to Virginia, whose captain was acquainted with Gonzalo: they saluted, and the French captain came on board; where seeing Monsieur Belanger, he appeared very joyful. "Sir," said he, "I have a lady on board, who has left France to follow you, the charming Madamoiselle Genevieve Santerell, your guardian's daughter, who sensible of the injuries her father has done you, and constant in her affection to you, is a passenger in my ship: I will go fetch her." Belanger stood like one thunder-struck at this news, and Charlotta looked upon him with disdain and shame; whilst joy glowed in Don Antonio de Medenta's face. And now it is fit that we should know the unfortunate maid's story, who thus followed him that fled from her.

CHAPTER 7

You have been already informed that this young lady was Monsieur Belanger's guardian's daughter, and by consequence his first cousin; they had been bred up together and designed for one another. She was fair, wise and virtuous, but yet could not charm Belanger's heart though he did hers; she loved him before she was sensible what love was, and her passion increased with her years. Her father did not fail to approve her choice, because it secured the estate to the family, and Belanger treated her always with much respect and tenderness as his kinswoman and a lady of great merit, but declined all promises of marriage; she was but little younger than himself, and had refused many advantageous offers, declaring she was pre-engaged.

She was much concerned at her father's wicked designs against him, and though she too well perceived he did not love her as a lover ought, which indeed her father hated him for, yet she so doted on him that she resolved to serve and follow him to death, flattered herself that since she could not discover any other person, time and her constancy would gain her his affection. When he left France to go for Virginia, she resolved to follow him so soon as she could get an opportunity, in order to which she got what money she could together, and went disguised like a man on board this French ship, where she made herself known to the captain, having left a letter for her father to acquaint him where she was gone.

She soon came aboard the Spanish ship, and seeing Belanger, who could not possibly receive her uncivilly, she ran to him with a transport that too well manifested her affection for him. "Are we again met," said she, "and has Heaven heard my vows? Nothing but death shall separate me from you any more."

"Madam," said he extremely disordered, "I am sorry that you have risked your life and honor so greatly for a person who is unable to make you the grateful returns you merit; my friendship shall ever speak my gratitude: but here is a lady to whom my faith is engaged. Too constant Genevive, how is my soul divided between love and gratitude!"

At these words Charlotta, who was inflamed with jealousy and distrust, seeing how beautiful her rival was, and reflecting that they had been long acquainted and bred up together, that it was his interest to marry the French lady, addressed herself to her in this manner, "Madam, your plea and title to his heart is of much older date than mine; it is just he should be yours and that I may convince you that my soul is generous and noble, I will save him the confusion of making apologies to me, and resign my right in him. Yes, base, ungenerous Belanger who have deceived me, return to your duty, I will no more listen to your oaths and vows, leave me to the providence of God; I ask no other favor of you and this lady, but to assist me to get a passage home to England."

Belanger was so confounded, he knew not what to do; he strove all he could to convince Charlotta of his sincerity, and at the same time not quite to drive a lady to despair for whom he had a tender regard. Madam Santerell, too sensible that he did not love her, and distracted to see her rival so adored, and herself so slighted and exposed, did all she was able to augment her rival's uneasiness; and now Belanger was so watched and teased by both, that he was at his wit's end. He desired to go into the French ship with the two ladies to go for Virginia, but

Don Medenta secretly opposed it, resolving to take Charlotta from him.

In order to which he got the Spanish captain to get Belanger to go on board the French ship to be merry, which he suspecting nothing did, leaving the two ladies sitting together in the great cabin. In some time after the Spanish captain stepping out of the room goes into his boat, and returning to his own ship, whispers Madam Santerell, whom Don Medenta and he had acquainted with their design, and who had willingly agreed to rid herself of her rival, to go on board the French ship immediately, which she did.

In the mean time Belanger missing Gonzalo, asked for him, and was told he was gone to his own ship, at which he was surprised; but when he saw the boat come back with one woman only, his color changed, and knowing Madam Santerell when she came nearer, he began to suspect some treachery; he gave her his hand to come into the ship, saying, "Where is Charlotta that you are come alone?"

"I have brought your trunks and things," said she, "because she is coming on board when the boat returns."

Whilst they were talking the boat made off, the trunks being handed up. He stormed like a madman, calling for the French captain's boat: mean time the Spanish ship made off with all her sails, being a ship of war and a good sailer, which the little merchant-ship, which was heavy laden, could not pretend to overtake. Having thus lost the divine Charlotta, whom he loved as much as man could love, he lost all patience, reproaching Madam Santerell in the most cruel terms, nay even cursing her as the cause of his ruin and death; whilst she endeavored to appease him with all the tender soft expressions imaginable, pretending that she was innocent and knew nothing of the Spaniard's design.

"Ah! cruel Belanger," said she, "do not repay my affection with such unkind treatment: have I not followed you, and left my native country, and all that was dear to me, exposing myself to all the dangers of the seas and various sicknesses incident to change of climates: In fine, what have I not done to merit your esteem? And are these the returns you make me? Must a stranger rob me of your heart? Consider what this usage may reduce me to do: If fate to punish you, has taken her from you, must I bear the blame? It is just Heaven, that in pity to my sufferings decrees your separation; and if you cannot love me, yet it is the least you can do to use me civilly and send me back to my home, that I may retire to some convent, and spend my unhappy life in prayers for you, for I will pray for and love you to death."

At these words she fainted and fell down at his feet. Belanger touched with this moving sight, almost forgot his own griefs, and laying her on his bed in his cabin, revived her with wine and cordials; and seeing her open her eyes, he took her kindly by the hand, saying, "Charming Genevive, forgive me the rash expressions I have used: urged by my despair I knew not what I did or said. I own the obligation I have to you, and have all the grateful sense of it that you can wish; you are dear to me as the ties of blood and friendship can make you, and though fate has permitted me to give my heart to another, yet you shall ever be the next to her in my esteem."

These tender speeches, with many others of the same kind, in some sort comforted the afflicted lady, who concluded in herself that she should in time, having got rid of her rival, get his affection; in order to which she behaved herself so towards him, and treated him with such respect and tenderness, that he was obliged to conceal his grief for Charlotta's loss, and appear tolerably satisfied. Yet he was almost distracted in reality, and determined to go in search of her so soon as he could get ashore at Virginia, and find a ship to carry him to the Island of St. Domingo, to which he knew the Spanish ship was bound, designing to leave Madam Santerell with his uncle.

Thus resolved he seemed pacified, and in few days they got into the desired port, and were received by his uncle with much joy. He promised upon hearing his nephew's story, to assist him in all he was able, to oblige his guardians in France to do him and his sister justice. And now Monsieur Belanger's whole business was, to get a bark to carry him to the island where he supposed his mistress to be; but the inward grief of his mind, and the constraint he had put upon himself, had so impaired his health, that he fell sick of a fever, which brought him so low that he was ten months before he was able to go out of his chamber, his illness being much increased by the vexation of his mind: all which time Madam de Santerell waited on and tended him with such extraordinary care and tenderness, that she much injured her own constitution, and fell into a consumption, at which Monsieur Belanger was much concerned.

In this time he contracted a great friendship with a young gentleman, his uncle's only son, a young man of extraordinary parts and goodness, handsome and ingenious; his name was Lewis de Montandre, which was the name of Monsieur de Belanger's mother's family: He was about twenty two years old, and had traveled most parts of Europe. To him Monsieur Belanger made known all his secret thoughts, and design of going to St. Domingo in search of Charlotta, and he offered to accompany him thither and to assist him in all he was able to. And here we must leave Monsieur Belanger to recover his health, and relate what befell Charlotta, who was left in Seignior de Medenta's hands and power.

CHAPTER 8

When she found the ship under sail and saw that she was betrayed and robbed of Belanger, she retired to her cabin, cast herself on her bed, and abandoned herself to grief. "My God," said she, lifting up her delicate hands and watery eyes, "for what am I reserved? What further misfortunes must I suffer? No sooner did thy providence provide me a friend to comfort me in my distress, and delivered me out of the merciless hands of pirates, but it has again exposed me helpless and alone to strangers, men who are more violent and revengeful in their natures than any I have yet met withal. Perhaps poor Belanger is already drowned in the merciless sea by the cruel Medenta, to whom, unless thy goodness again delivers me, I must be a sacrifice."

Whilst she was thus expostulating with Heaven, the amorous Spaniard came to her cabin-door, and gently opening it, sat down on the bed by her, and seeing her drowned in tears, was for some moments silent. At last, taking her hand he kissed it passionately, and said, "Too charming lovely maid, why do you thus abandon yourself to passion? Give me leave to convince you that you have no just cause of grief, and that I have done nothing base or dishonourable; your lover had ungratefully left a lady to whom he had been engaged from his infancy, one who highly deserved his esteem, and so loved him that you see she has ventured her life and fame to follow him. To you he was a stranger, and being false to her he had known so long, you have all the reason in the world to doubt his constancy to you. Your rival had resolved to rid herself of you, and you were hourly in danger of death whilst she was with you. Believe me, Charlotta, the fear of losing you whom my soul adores, made me take such measures to secure your life, and restore to the lady her faithless lover.

"I am disengaged, and have a fortune worthy your acceptance. This day, this hour, if you will consent, I will marry you to secure you from all fears of being ruined or abandoned by me; and till you permit me to be happy, I will guard and wait on you with such respect and assiduity, that you shall at last be constrained to own that I do merit to be loved, and with that lovely mouth confirm me happy."

She answered him with much reserve, wisely considering in herself, that if she treated him with too much rigor, he might be provoked to use other means to gratify his passion; that she was wholly in his power, and unable to deliver herself out of his hands. In fine, some days passed, in which she was so altered with grief, that her lover was under great concern, he treated her with all the gallantry and tender regard that a man could use to gain a lady's heart. He let nothing be wanting, but presented her with wines, sweetmeats, and everything the ship afforded, offering her gold and rings, and at length perceived that she grew more cheerful and obliging, at which he was even transported.

The weather had till now been very favourable; but as they were sailing near the Summer Islands, a dreadful storm or hurricane arose, and drove them with such fury for a day and a night, that the ship at last struck against one of the smallest of them, and stuck so fast on the shore that they could not get her off, which obliged them to get the boats out, and lighten the ship of the guns and heaviest things, in doing which they discovered that the ship had sprung a leak; this made them under a necessity of staying on this island for some days to repair the damage. The captain, Charlotta, Don Medenta, and all the ship's crew went on shore. They found it was one of those islands that was uninhabited, so that they resolved to go thence as soon as they could to Bermudas; but Providence had decreed their stay there for some time.

The night they landed, about midnight, the sky darkened extremely, and such a storm of lightning and thunder followed, that the ship took fire, and was consumed with all that was left in it. The affrighted Charlotta, who had no other covering to defend her but the tents they had made of the tarpaulins and sails, now thought her misfortunes and life were at an end; her lover and all the rest recommended themselves to God, not expecting to survive that dreadful night. Some of the ship's crew venturing to look out after the ship, were lost, being blown into the sea, and the morning showed the dismal prospect of their flaming ship, which lay burning on the shore almost entire consumed. All the hope they now had left, was that some boats or barks would come to their relief from the adjacent islands.

The storm being over towards evening, after having taken some refreshment of what provisions and drink they had left which they had brought on shore, they ventured to walk about the island, on which was plenty of fowl and trees. Don Medenta leading Charlotta, they wandered to a place where they saw some trees growing very close together, in the midst of which they perceived a sort of hut or cottage made of a few boards and branches of trees, and coming up to it saw a door standing open made of a hurdle of canes; and concluding this place was inhabited by somebody, curiosity induced them to look into it.

There, stretched on an old mattress, lay a man who appeared to be of a middle age, pale as death, and so meagre and motionless, that they doubted whether he was living or dead. His habit was all torn and ragged, yet there appeared something so lovely and majestic in his even dying look, that it nearly touched their souls. Don Medenta going into this poor hut, took him by the hand, and finding he was not dead, spoke to him, asking if he could rise and eat, who he was, and other questions, to all which he made no answer, but looked earnestly upon him. Meantime Charlotta ran and fetched a bottle of rum, returning with such incredible speed that only that ardent charity that inflamed her generous soul could have enabled her to do. Don Medenta poured some of this rum into his mouth, but it was some time before the poor creature could swallow it; at last he seemed a little revived, and said in French, "God preserve you who have relieved me." He could say no more, but fainted. Don Medenta repeating his charitable office, gave him more rum, whilst Charlotta fetched some bread and meat; he swallowed a mouthful or two, but could eat no more.

By this time the captain and other officers came up, and were equally surprised at so sad an object; two of the seamen were ordered to stay with him that night, and the next morning Charlotta and the rest returned to visit him, impatient to know who he was, and how he came in that condition. He was come a little to himself, and received them in so courtly a manner, though he was unable to rise up upon his feet his weakness was so great, that they concluded he was some man of quality; and after some civilities had passed, Don Medenta begged to know who he was. "I will," said he, "if I am able, oblige you with the recital of a story so full of wonders, that it will merit a place in your memories all the days of your lives; you seem to be gentlemen, and that young lady's curiosity shall be gratified." Don Medenta bowing, seated Charlotta and himself on the ground by him, the captain and the rest stood before the cottage-door; and the stranger having taken a piece of biscuit and a glass of wine, being very faint, began the narrative of his life in the following manner.

CHAPTER 9

I was born in France at St. Malos, my father was a rich merchant in that place, his name was du Pont, I was the youngest of two sons which he had, and being grown up to man's estate, my father was mighty solicitous to see me disposed of advantageously, hoping I should marry such a fortune as might provide for me without lessening his own, so that my elder brother might be advanced to a title which he designed to purchase for him, or some great employ. This he was continually rounding in my ears. But, alas, my soul was averse to his commands, for I had already engaged my affections to a young lady whom I had unfortunately seen when I was but fifteen, at a monastery to which I had been sent by my father, to see a kinswoman who was a professed nun there. Visiting her, I saw this fair young pensioner, who was then about fifteen years old. She was beautiful as an angel, and I found her conversation as charming as her face. Her name was Angelina: and the monastery being at a village not above ten miles distant from St. Malos.

I used secretly to visit her at least once or twice a week, so that I got her promise to marry me so soon as I was settled in the world. She told me she was the only daughter of an old widow lady who lived fifty miles distant, was extremely rich, and had placed her there, because the abbess was her mother's sister; that her fortune was left her at her mother's disposal. This was her circumstance, which obliged me, being a younger brother, to defer marrying her till I had got so provided for, that I might venture to take her without asking our parents' consent: and this delay was our undoing, for when I was twenty, an old widow-lady came to my father's on some money-affairs, and was lodged at our house, where she took such a fancy to me, that she boldly solicited my father to lay his commands upon me to marry her, which offer he readily accepted. And having laid all the advantages of this rich match before me, concluded with enjoining me with the strictest injunctions to marry her forthwith. I pleaded in vain that I was pre-engaged to another. He told me in a rage, I must take my choice, either to consent or go out of his doors immediately, protesting he would never give me a groat, and disown me if I was disobedient to his commands.

But when I proceeded in the humblest manner to make known who the person was to whom I was pre-engaged, good heavens! how was I surprised to find it was this lady's daughter? And now the fatal secret being known, Angelina was in few days removed out of my sight and knowledge, being taken away from the monastery, and sent I knew not where. Some months passed in which I busied myself in making inquiry after her, but all in vain. At last, quite wearied out with my father's threats and the widow's importunities, I consented to be wretched and married her, whom in my soul I loathed and hated, nor had I done it, but in hopes to get to the knowledge of the place where my dear Angelina was concealed from me, resolving never to consummate my marriage with her mother, which way of proceeding so enraged her, that we lived at continual variance; yet shame with-held her from declaring this secret to the world, together with spite, because she would continue to plague me by living with me.

At last, by the means of one of the servants, whom I bribed, (having now all her fortune at command, which I took care to manage so well, that I laid by a great sum of money to provide for me and Angelina, with whom I resolved to fly from France so soon as I could find her) I got knowledge that she was locked up in a convent near

Calais. On which I converted all my money secretly into gold and bills of exchange, resolving to set out for England with her so soon as we could get off, having there an uncle at Bristol, my father's brother. At these words Charlotta looked earnestly upon him, surprised to find he was her cousin-german. But he continued his discourse thus: "But now I was in a great dilemma how to get to the speech of her to inform her of my design, as likewise how to get away from my wife, who was continually hanging upon me and following me, fearing she should discover whither I was going, being certain she would remove Angelina from the convent. I therefore picked a quarrel one evening with my wife about a trifle on purpose, and the next morning took horse by break of day, attended with only one servant in whom I could confide, and set out for St. Malos, where being arrived, I hired a vessel to carry me to Calais, fearing to be followed if I had gone by land. The wind was contrary for some days, so that my revengeful wife had time to send for Angelina from the convent. At my arrival there, I had the mortification to find her gone, but none could, or indeed would, inform me whither she was carried: this so exasperated me against my wife, that I resolved not to return home any more.

So I went directly to my father's, and stayed there a month, pretending business with some masters of ships that were expected to come into that port. Meantime my wife got intelligence where I was, and came to me. I received her civilly before my father; but at night, when we were in bed, we fell into a warm dispute, which ended in a resolution on my side to leave her for ever, with which I acquainted her. But then she fell to entreaties, and in the softest terms laid before me my ingratitude to her, and how wicked my design was upon her daughter; pleading, that as she was my wife, she had all the reason in the world to keep me from the conversation of a person whom I loved better than herself; that she had made me master of a plentiful fortune, and concealed from the world the high affront I had put upon her, in refusing to perform the duties of a husband to her. To all which I answered, that as for the ceremony of our marriage, I looked upon it as nothing, since I was compelled to it; that I had denied myself all converse with her as a wife, because I would not commit a sin, by breaking my solemn vows and engagements with her daughter, whom I had made choice of before I saw her; and since there was no other way left to free me, I resolved to declare all to the world, and annul our marriage, and restore what money and estate I had remaining in my hands to her. At these words she flew into a violent passion. "Well then," said she, "since you will thus expose me, I'll do myself this justice, to remove Angelina from your sight for ever; be assured you shall never see her more in this world." She that moment leaped out of bed, called for her servant, and put on her clothes; and though I used many entreaties to deter her, nay proceeded to threats, yet she persisted in her resolution, and going down to my father, acquainted him with all that had passed between us, desiring him to prevent me from following her, which he, being highly incensed against me, too well performed: for he came up to my chamber, where I was dressing in order to follow her, but he kept me there in discourse whilst she took coach and was gone I knew not whither, nor could I for some days hear any news of her.

Meantime my father and brother continually persecuted me on her account, bidding me go home and live like a Christian; nay they employed several priests and the bishop of the place to talk to me, so that I was now looked on with much dislike; and being weary of this schooling, I set out for home, where I found my wife sick, which indeed so touched me, that I repented of having used her so unkindly, and resolved to treat her more respectfully for the time to come. A whole year passed, all which time she languished of a lingering fever and inward decay, grief having doubtless seized her spirits. I used her with as much tenderness as if I had been her son. We never bedded together, but kept two apartments. In fine, she died, and on her death-bed, some hours before she expired, took me by the hand as I sat on her bedside, and said these words to me, which are still fresh in my memory: "Du Pont, I am now going to leave you, and I hope to be at rest. I have loved you as tenderly and passionately as ever wife did a husband; and though I committed a great folly in marrying a person who was so much younger than myself, and pre-engaged, yet no vicious inclinations induced me to it, as my behaviour to you since must convince you. I flattered myself, that gratitude and my behaviour towards you, would have gained your love, but was deceived. I have never been to blame in all my conduct towards you, but to my child I have been cruel and unkind; for fearing a criminal conversation between you if you came together, I used all my endeavours to keep you asunder, and finding that even the convents could not secure her, provoked by your ill usage, at last I resolved to send her out of France, which I effected by means of a captain of a ship which was bound to Canada, who took her with him with a sum of money, promising to see her there disposed of in marriage to some merchant or officer in those parts, which we doubted not but she would readily consent to, finding herself among strangers, and bereft of all hopes of seeing you any more. I have never heard of her since. This action I heartily repent of, and to expiate my fault, I shall leave you all my fortune, with a strict injunction, as you hope for everlasting happiness hereafter, to go in search of her, and employ it in endeavouring to find her; and if she be married, give her part to make her happy: and may that God, whose merciful forgiveness and pardon I now implore, direct and prosper you, and bring you safe together, if she be yet single. I can do no more, but ask you to accept of this my last action as an atonement for all the trouble I have occasioned you, and not hate my memory." I was so struck with hearing Angelina was sent so far off, and so disarmed of my resentments by the sight of my wife's condition, who was now struggling with death, that the tears poured down my face, and my soul was so oppressed, that I swooned. Which so disturbed her, that her confessor, who was present at this discourse, ordered me to be carried out of the room." Here he seemed faint, and Don Medenta gave him some wine; after which he continued his relation in this manner. "Recovering from my swoon, I soon discovered by the outcries and lamentations of the servants that my wife was dead.

I behaved myself with all the decency and prudence I was able on this occasion, and buried her suitable to her birth and fortune; after which I thought of nothing but my voyage to Canada, having informed myself of the ship and captain's name, who carried away

Angelina; which was not returned, or expected back to France in three years, being gone a trading voyage for some merchants at Diep. I left my father to take care of the estate, who sent my brother to reside there; made my will, and having provided myself with money, bills of exchange, and all other necessaries, I went aboard a merchant ship called the Venturous, bound for those parts to trade, not doubting but that we should meet with the captain there who had conveyed Angelina thither, and then there was no question but I should make him confess where he had left her. We had a prosperous voyage for some weeks, but coming near Newfoundland, we unfortunately met a pirate-ship who boarded and took us after a fierce dispute which lasted three hours, in which our ship was so shattered, that she sunk as they were rifling of her. In this accident several of the pirates perished, and all the passengers and sailors belonging to our ship, except my unfortunate self and surgeon, who were taken up by ropes into the pirate ship, where we were put in irons into the hold, I suppose because they were in an ill humour at the loss of their companions and the ship.

Some days passed before we had the favour of being brought up upon the deck, and our irons taken off. We were both very sick; as for my part, I was so afflicted at being prevented from going my intended voyage, that I was careless of what became of me. There was amongst the pirates some that looked like gentlemen, but they all talked and behaved themselves like desperate villains, oaths and curses were as common as in a gaming-house, they drank like Germans, and discoursed like atheists and libertines: they asked us many questions, who and what we were, to all which we answered cautiously. I told them, if they would set me on any shore thereabouts, from whence I might travel by land, or get shipping to Canada, I would promise if I lived to return to France, to remit a thousand pistoles to any part of the world, or person they should name; they took little notice of my offers, but let us have the liberty of walking in the day-time on the decks, and at night they put us under hatches. At last we arrived at the island of Providence, where they were received by their companions with much joy. We remained in this wretched place ten whole months, in which time they used us like slaves, with many others whom they could not prevail with to take up their desperate manner of living.

At last, wearied with this way of life, we desired to go out in one of their ships, desiring them to treat us as we should deserve by our bravery and good behaviour. They consented; and now all my hopes were that I should meet a welcome death to free me from the miseries of life, or find some way to escape from them. There were beside myself and friend, six gentlemen, three of whom were Spaniards, and the other three English, who, like us, went with them through necessity. The ship was a frigate of 30 guns, and carried 140 hands: they designed to cruise near the Havana, in hopes to catch some of the Spanish ships coming out thence. As we lay cruising at some distance, a dreadful storm arose, which at last tore our ship in pieces near this island where we now are. Every man was obliged to shift for himself; I caught hold of a plank, floating on which, it pleased Providence to cause the winds and waves to cast me on this place much bruised.

Here I have been three weeks. I made this hut with some old planks and what I found on the shore, to secure me from the cold and storms. This old mattress and coat I also found. All my food has been the eggs of sea-fowls and birds, which I have daily gathered up on the sands and in holes in the rocks and hollow trees. But the anguish of my mind, with the bruises I received in my stomach in the shipwreck, had at last reduced me to such weakness, that I could no longer rise on my feet to seek for food. And when divine providence brought you here to my relief, I had been three whole days without tasting any sustenance, and had by this been freed from my miseries." Then he fetched a deep sigh, concluding his story with these words: "Yet I am in duty bound to thank God and you, and hope, since he has prolonged my stay on earth a little longer, that he will make life supportable, by furnishing me with means to find her out, without whom I must be ever wretched."

And now Charlotta acquainted him who she was, and in few words of the manner of her coming to that place. At which he was filled with admiration; but he was so amazed when he heard that

Monsieur Belanger and Madam de Santerel had left France in such a manner, that he could scarce credit it, they being his intimate friends. Yet she in the relation spared to mention Don Medenta's treachery, or Belanger's love to her, saying only he was gone to Virginia in a French ship. And now the conversation turning to be general, every person spoke their sentiments of du Pont's adventures. Some days passed with much anxiety, provisions were husbanded, and their fears of wanting daily increased; yet du Pont mended, and company rendered their solitary way of living in this desolate place more supportable. They were hourly in expectation of seeing some ship pass by to the adjacent islands, having placed a white cloth on the top of a stick on the most eminent part of the island, to give notice of their distress: thus they spent three whole weeks, in which time most of the victuals they had saved were spent, and the dreadful apprehensions of famine appeared in every face, and every one walked about looking what they could find to eat, in hopes to satisfy nature without diminishing the small stock of provisions they had left.

Don Medenta, who was one of the most vigilant in searching out something to give Charlotta fit for her to eat, went one morning to the farthest part of the island, which was about seven miles over, and there ascending a high rock, stood looking on the sea, and saw a boat fastened in a little cliff of the rock, out of which cliff a Blackamoor man came, and launching out the boat, put off to sea, making towards another island. Don Medenta concluded this person lived somewhere in this rock, and resolved to search about it in hopes to discover some persons there, by whom he might be assisted and his friends, to get from this dismal island, or at least to wait the man's return, or find out his abode, in order to return thither that evening. He found it very dangerous to descend on that side of the rock next the sea, and was long ere he could find the place out of which he saw the man come forth; but at last he perceived a sort of a door, which seemed to shut in a place that was the entrance of a cavern in the rock: but it was fast locked, and he could not discern through the key-hole anything but a glimmering light, yet he heard a human voice like a woman's, talking to a child, but he understood but little of it, because it was a language he could not speak much of, being English. He waited some hours, but finding the man did not return, he went away, and hastened to Charlotta with the glad tidings that he had found a boat, and persons on the island. Both she and the whole company were agreeably surprised with this news; and the captain, Monsieur du Pont, Don Medenta and Charlotta, all resolved to make their evening's walk to this place.

CHAPTER 10

ccording to the resolution taken in the morning, Charlotta
and the rest walked to the rock in the evening, and getting
up to the top of it, saw from thence the black man standing
at the entrance of his cave, with a white woman who seemed to be
very young and very handsome; she had a mulatto child in her arms
about a year old, her gown and petticoat was made of a fine silk. Don
Medenta called to them in French, at which the man looked up; and
Charlotta spoke in English to the woman, desiring her to come up and
speak to her; on which the blackamoor pushed the woman in, and
returning no answer, shut the door upon himself and her.

Don Medenta and the rest concluded, that they feared being
discovered; so they all descended the rock and went to the door,
resolving to force it open if they could not gain entrance otherwise,
and remove their fears by speaking gently to them, and acquainting
them with their distress. They knocked and called at the door for
some time; but hearing a noise within, and no answer, they broke
open the door with much difficulty, and entering, went through a
narrow passage in the rock, so strait that but one person could go
abreast; at the end of which they came into some strange rooms fashioned by nature, though cleansed of mess and loose stones by labor.

Into these, light entered by the holes that were in some places open through the top of the rocks; but some part of the caves, or caverns (for they were scarce fit to be called rooms) were very dark.

In the biggest room was a lamp burning, and here they saw two chests locked, and on a shelf some platters and bowls made of calabash-shells, with two or three wooden spits; and some sticks were burning in a corner of the room, in a place made with stones piled round, and opening in the front like a furnace, on which stood a pot, wherein something was boiling. There likewise hung up some fishing-tackle and a gun with a powder-horn, as also a bow with a quiver of arrows. In a place which was shut with a door, like a cupboard, stood bread and flour, and on the table (for there was a very odd one, and stools, which seemed to be of the Negro's own making) stood a basket with some clean linen for a child, and some canvas cut out for slaves' jackets and drawers. In another room they saw a quilt and coverlets lying on some rushes on the floor; but they could find no living creature, at which they were much amazed.

They called, and spoke in the softest terms, desiring them to come forth, if hid there, promising to do them no harm; but in vain. At last they heard a child cry, and following the sound of the voice, went through a narrow turning on the right hand, which brought them to a place where a door was shut, before which lay a terrible bear. Don Medenta, who was the foremost, carrying the lamp in one hand, and his sword in the other, being presently more apprehensive of Charlotta's danger than his own, she being next behind him, ran at the bear, designing to kill it, if possible, before it could rise; but was stopped by the sound of a human voice which came from that beast, saying, "For Heaven's sake, spare my life, and I'll do all you'll have me."

At these words the Negro came out of the bear's skin, and threw himself at Medenta's feet, who took him up; and Charlotta bid him fear nothing, they being persons in distress, that wanted his assistance, and would pay him nobly for serving them. Then he opened the door he had lain before in the beast's skin, and brought forth the young woman and child, whom Charlotta embraced, whilst the poor creature wept for joy to see a Christian white man. And now they were all cheerful, and the Negro being told, that they wanted nothing but his assistance, to carry one of them to any of the adjacent islands that was inhabited to get them some provisions, and hire a vessel to carry them to the Island of St. Domingo, he readily promised to do it.

"My boat," said he, "will carry no great weight, being a small canoe which I made myself; but it will carry me and one more, with some small quantity of provisions." And now they were all impatient to know how this beautiful woman and black man came to this place; which they found she seemed not willing to declare whilst the Negro was present: and therefore Charlotta begged that she might accompany her whilst he brought the boat round to the other side of the island, to take in one of the sailors; not thinking it safe to trust Don Medenta, or one of the gentlemen with him, in so slight a vessel. This the Negro did not seem to be pleased withal, but yet dared not refuse it. He used to drag his boat up out of the water into a cleft, where it was impossible to be seen. And now the transported woman, with her tawny child, accompanied Charlotta to her tent, and in the way recounted her sad story in these words.

"My name is Ifabinda. I am the daughter of a planter in Virginia, who has a great plantation there, is extremely rich; and having no more daughters than myself, bred me up in the best manner, sending me to England for education, from whence I returned at thirteen years old. I was courted by several, and by one in particular whom I liked, and my father did not disapprove of; but it was my unhappy fate to be miserably disappointed of all my hopes. Amongst a great many Negro-slaves whom my father had to work in our plantation, he you saw was one, who appearing to be bred above the rest, and more capable of being serviceable in the house, was taken into it.

He was about twenty years old, handsome and witty, could read and write, having (as he pretends) been a prince in his own country, and taught several languages and arts by a Romish priest, who was cast ashore at Angola, from whence he came. He behaved himself so well, that he gained my father's favor, and used often to wait on me when I walked out in an evening, or rode out, running by my horse's side; in short, he was ever ready to do me service. We had a pleasure-boat, having a city-house at James-Town; and when I was there, I used often, with my companions, to go on the water in the evenings for pleasure, and then he used to steer the boat. He made himself the little boat you saw here, on pretence to go out a fishing for me, which much pleased my father, the fashion and usefulness of it being extraordinary; for it sails swift, and bears a rough sea beyond any thing we had ever seen. He used to catch fish very dexterously, as he did every thing he went about: He could paint, understood navigation, the mathematics; and in short, was so beloved by my father, that he would have freed him, had he not feared losing of him.

And now Domingo, for that is his name, became enamored with me, and lift up his aspiring eyes to my unhappy face: His passion increased with time, and at last he resolved to possess me, or die in the attempt. Had he but once given me the least intimation of his passion, I should have acquainted my father with his insolence, and his death would have prevented my ruin: but this he knew, and therefore so well kept the secret to himself, that no body suspected it. He had taken care to provide some bread and money, by selling some tobacco, and little mathematical instruments and pictures he had made, my father having given him a little piece of ground to plant, to buy him linen, allowing him to go finer dressed than other slaves. He also permitted him, when we went to the town, to sell trifles that he made.

In fine, he waited only an opportunity to get me into his little boat, which he thus effected: One evening, the sea being very calm, he sat in the boat a fishing, having hid the bread and money in it; I walking down with my maid, to see what he had caught for my supper, he persuaded me to step into the boat, and sit down. 'Now, Madam,' said he, 'you shall see sport.' He was pulling in a little net; I sat down, and the maid stood on the shore. He, in dragging the net, loosed the boat from the shore, which beginning to drive out to sea, surprised me; but he bid me sit still, and fear nothing. I sat very patient for some time, till at last seeing him hoist the sail, and go farther from land, I began to be frightened; he pretended to be so too, and persuaded me he could not help it, that the wind and stream drove the boat against his will. He pulled a little compass out of his pocket, by which he steered. We were two nights and days thus sailing, in which time we passed by some islands, on which he pretended he could not land, because, as I since discovered, he knew they were inhabited, and had before marked out this desolate place to carry me to.

At last he brought me hither half dead with the fright, and faint, having eat only a little of the bread, and drank out of a bottle of wine which he had in the boat, in which he had put his tools for making mathematical instruments, and colors for painting. When we were landed, he seemed mighty solicitous where to find a place for me to lie down, and food for me; and brought me into the cavern in the rock: There being seated on his jacket, on the ground, we eat what fish he had in the boat, broiled on a fire he made with sticks, having a tinder-box in his pocket. After we had eat he told me his design. 'My dear lady,' said he, 'I love you to madness, and was resolved to possess you or die: Though my outside is black, and distasteful, I fear, to your eyes, yet my soul is as noble and lovely as your own. I was born a prince, and free; and though chance made me a slave, and the barbarous Christians bought and sold me, yet my mind they never could subdue. I adore you, and have long designed what I have now effected. No human creature dwells here besides ourselves, and from this place you never must expect to return.' Here he proceeded to kiss me, my distraction was such, that I swooned; he took the advantage of those unhappy minutes, when I was unable to resist, and, in fine, has kept me here two whole years, maintaining me by carrying what he makes to the adjacent islands; where he sells his ingenious work to the inhabitants, and brings back provisions and clothes for us: from thence he brought all you see in our miserable habitation; and to employ me, he brings work from these people. I make clothes for the slaves, and by this means, and his fishing and shooting, we have food enough.

I had a pearl necklace, and some rings in my ears and on my fingers, of value, when he brought me here; which he sold, and traded with the money. I have had but this child by him, which he doats on. He is a Christian, and would gladly marry me. He is so jealous, that whenever he discovers any body landed on the island, he always locks me up, if he goes out; and lives in continual fear, lest my father should make any discovery where we are, and send some to take me from him; in case of which I believe he would certainly kill me. He told me of your being here some days since, and warned me not to venture forth; which indeed I longed to do, in hopes to meet with somebody to converse withal, being weary of living such a solitary miserable life. When he found you were resolved to enter our being, which he thought secure, he put me into the room you saw me in, and placed himself before it in the bear's skin; a stratagem he had invented long before, supposing no body would venture to search farther, when they saw so terrible a creature in so dismal a place. He had stuffed the legs, feet and head of the beast; so that placing himself in the belly of it, it appeared alive, especially in so dark a place. The two large chests you saw, he found on the shore some months since, in which there are much rich clothes, linen and treasure, the spoils of some unhappy ship that was doubtless shipwrecked on this coast.

And now I have acquainted you with all my unhappy story, and must implore your assistance to persuade Domingo to leave this place, and take us with you, or else help me to escape from him; though I would now willingly consent to be his wife, having treasure sufficient to purchase us a good settlement in any place. If he be ever found by any body from Virginia, my father will surely put him to death, but Domingo will kill me first; and to live thus is worse than death."

Here she wept, and Charlotta embracing her, promised never to part with her. "No, my dear Ifabinda," said she, "we will part no more; Domingo shall be carried hence to the place we are bound to, where he may safely and lawfully possess you; since you now love, as I perceive, and have forgiven him his crime in getting you, we will assist him to be happy. The selling human creatures, is a crime my soul abhors; and wealth so got, never thrives. Though he is black, yet the Almighty made him as well as us, and Christianity never taught us cruelty: We ought to visit those countries to convert, not buy our fellow-creatures, to enslave and use them as if we were devils, or they not men."

Don Medenta joined with her in opinion; and the captain and all agreed to have them married, and take them along with them. And now being come to their tent, they sat down to eat, poor Ifabinda being so transported with such charming conversation, that Charlotta could not refrain from praising God in her heart, for sending her such a sweet companion.

CHAPTER 11

About the close of the day Domingo returned with the sailor, with the joyful tidings that there was a Spanish ship at the island they had been at, and that the captain had promised to come the next morning in his long-boat to fetch them away, his name being Don Manuel des Escalado, a particular friend of Gonzalo's and Don Medenta's. This news revived them all, and now Charlotta talked to Domingo, offering him to take him and Isabinda to St. Domingo, and see them married in the Spanish ship the next day: and Don Medenta promised that the governor his father should permit them to settle there; and then, said he, Ifabinda may, if you think fit, write to her father, and let him know where she is.

Domingo gladly accepted of this proposal, being so overjoyed to hear that Ifabinda consented to marry him, that he fell prostrate on the ground, and returned thanks to God in so passionate a manner, that it moved all the company. But Charlotta being still deeply concerned for the loss of Belanger, seeing herself going to be carried to a place where she should be no longer able to resist Don Medenta's desires, where his father commanded every thing, and from whence there was no possibility to escape without his knowledge; a place where she must either yield to be Medenta's mistress, or wife, and should be necessitated to break her vows and faith given to Belanger; resolved to try the force of her eloquence and power over Medenta, to prevail with him to land her at Virginia, or at least give her his faithful promise to send her thither by the first ship that went from St. Domingo.

In order to this, she asked him to walk with her alone a little way that evening, which he gladly did; and then he began to break her mind to him in the most soft and moving terms imaginable: "Though we are not of one religion," said she, "yet we are both Christians; I have given my faith to another, how can I be yours without a crime? I have all the grateful sense that I ought of your civilities towards me, and wish my heart had not been pre-engaged, that I might have been yours; but since I cannot break through my engagements with him, permit me to be just, and be assured that I will ever love and esteem you next himself whilst I live. He will undoubtedly come to St. Domingo to look after me; and with what confusion shall I see him, when married to you? Besides, your father and family will abhor me as beneath you; it is altogether unfit for you to marry a poor English maid, whose family and education you are a stranger to, and who has no fortune to recommend her to the honor of being your wife; so that should I consent, we must be wretched."

Don Medenta returned this answer: "Lovely Charlotta, on whom I have placed all my love, and in whom my whole happiness in this life consists, I can no more consent to part with you than with my hopes of future happiness, or my faith. It is impossible for me to live without you; Belanger merits not your love, he is false to another, and with him you must expect a curse: besides, it is in vain to dispute, I am resolved never to part with you: I have a father who is so tender of me, and so generous and good in his nature, that he will be glad to see me happy, and be fond of you, because you are mine; my family will follow his example; I have a sister fair and wise as yourself, she loves me dearly, and shall be your companion and friend: Your virtue is a portion, and I have wealth enough to make us happy; and, to remove all obstacles, you shall not set your foot out of the ship we are designed to go on board of tomorrow morning, till I have wedded and bedded you; which if you consent not to, I must first bed, and then marry you, for you are in my power, must and shall be mine; and by this gentle compulsion, I'll remove your scruples, and acquit you of your promises to the treacherous Belanger, my now hated rival."

At these words he let go her hand in a kind of disorder, and walked hastily back towards the tent. She followed, much distracted in her thoughts; he stayed till she overtook him, but went along with her home without speaking another word. After supper, Charlotta retiring to bed, could not close her eyes all night; and having in that time well weighed and considered all he said, resolved to consent to marry him, choosing rather to yield to be his with honor, than reduce him to treat her in a manner she dreaded worse than death. Madam de Santerell's following Belanger, and his negligence, as she construed it, in going into the French ship, and leaving her behind, had a little piqued her; and her circumstances, being in Medenta's hands, obliged her to agree to be his; nor did she dislike him, he was beautiful, had a great fortune, was nobly born, and finely bred. She rose, determined to compose her thoughts, and, if possible, banish the passion she had for Belanger out of her soul; but that was impossible.

Don Medenta next morning appeared with an unusual gravity in his looks; the long-boat soon arrived with the Spanish captain, and all the gentlemen he had on board, and was received very joyfully; all things worth carrying away were already packed up by the diligent sailors, and soon sent aboard; and then the boat returning in the evening, Don Medenta, Charlotta, Ifabinda, the Moor Domingo, Monsieur du Pont, Gonzalo, and all the rest went into it, bidding adieu to the desolate island, and arrived safe to the ship, where they were welcomed with the guns and good wine.

The next morning they weighed anchor, and the ship set sail for the Island of St. Domingo; then Don Medenta earnestly solicited Charlotta to marry him, and was seconded by Mons. de Pont, and the good father who was chaplain to the ship, a friar whose name was Ignatinis, to whom he had declared his reasons and resolutions; at last she yielded, and was that day married, as was also Ifabinda to her amorous Moor, who on this occasion behaved himself so handsomely, and expressed such satisfaction and transport, that every body was charmed with him.

In few hours they reached the island, and then Charlotta was conducted by Don Medenta to his father's castle, where she was surprised at the great attendance and sumptuous furniture; the governor received his son with great joy and affection, and when he presented Charlotta to him, begging his blessing and pardon for marrying without his consent, he took her up and embraced her, saying, "If she be as virtuous as fair, which I doubt not, since you have made her your wife, and be a Catholick, I not only give you my blessing, but will do all that is necessary to make you great and happy." Here Charlotta was surprised, being a Protestant, and was ready to sink; but Don Medenta, squeezing her by the hand to give her a hint to conceal her disorder, replied briskly, "Honored Sir, she is all you can desire, virtuous, wise, pious, and will I am certain be an honor and comfort to us both."

Then Don Medenta's sister, the charming Teresa, a most accomplished young lady, coming into the presence-chamber, welcomed her brother and new sister, to whom she made a present of some very rich jewels she had on. And now all the court (for so the governor's palace was justly called, for he was there as great, and lived like a king) was soon crowded with all the principal gentlemen and merchants in the town; a mighty treat was got ready, the bells were set a ringing, and after the supper there was a great ball; Charlotta was so complimented and caressed, and her friend Ifabinda, who accompanied her as a companion attendant, her circumstance not being mentioned, that she was astonished; and being so young, and unused to such greatness, no doubt but she at this instant forgot Belanger, and was transported at her good fortune in getting so noble a husband as Don Medenta.

The ball ended, she was by her husband conducted to a most splendid apartment, attended by her father-in-law, sister, and all the company. Here being again complimented, the company took leave, and an old lady with two waiting women, waited on her and Ifabinda into a dressing-room, into which none but Teresa entered with them;

the old lady undressed her, the servants put her on a rich laced suit of night-clothes, a delicate fine shift, night-gown and petticoats; all which Teresa furnished for her new sister, whose beauty she much admired, and highly respected her brother. Ifabinda had a fine suit of night-clothes, night-gown and petticoats given her also, and a chamber prepared next Charlotta's to lie in. Charlotta was conducted by Teresa to a bed-chamber, where the bed was a rich brocade, the hangings arras, and every thing magnificent beyond any thing she had ever seen in her life. So soon as she was in bed, Teresa and the rest took leave; then Don Medenta came in at another door in his night-gown, and went to bed to her: mean time the governor dismissed the company, and retired to his apartment.

Now it is fit that we inform ourselves where Gonzalo and the rest of the passengers were disposed of; he and Domingo and the officers belonging to the ship, stayed on board to see the ship cleared and laid up in the harbor, Don Medenta having not thought it proper the Moor should appear with Ifabinda till he had acquainted his father with their story; and therefore it was resolved that he should come to the governor's the next morning with the captain, who was obliged to wait on him, and give an account of his voyage every time he returned from sea; Domingo's two chests, in which was all his wealth, were to be likewise brought to the castle: the Moor, who was much inclined to jealousy, passed the night very ill, and thought the time long till the rising sun appeared; he had his little boy a-bed with him, whom he hugged and kissed all night; and rising at day-break, took a rich habit out of one of his chests, and dressed himself like a petty-prince, as he really was by birth in his own country; he likewise put a rich cloak on little Domingo, which Ifabinda had made him with some scarlet cloth and silver-lace, the Moor had brought her for that purpose from the islands he used to trade to. Thus he waited, ready to attend the captain and Monsieur du Pont to the castle, to which they went about ten o'clock, by which time Don Medenta was risen, and had acquainted his father with Ifabinda's story and du Pont's; the governor welcomed them all, Domingo he embraced, and promised him his protection and favor. Don Medenta conducted him to Ifabinda and

Charlotta, who were together in their apartment entertaining a great many ladies, who were come to pay their compliments and breakfast with them.

And now nothing but feasting and joy were thought on by all but these two ladies, who having been both bred Protestants, were in a great consternation how they should behave themselves. Charlotta had reasoned that morning with her lord on this subject, and he had convinced her that she was under a necessity of dissembling her religion; for if his father and family discovered she was a Protestant, she must expect to be hated and slighted, nay that he should be ruined, and perhaps parted from her. These thoughts almost distracted her, and she had communicated them secretly to Ifabinda when she came into her chamber in the morning; they both wept, and found too late they must be of their husbands' religion, or be wretched. Charlotta even repented her breach of faith with Belanger, and began to apprehend the misfortunes that the change which she had made would bring upon her; but she concealed her thoughts, and they went to mass every day, which made them highly caressed by the whole court, and much obliged their husbands.

Domingo, who was impatient to retire with his wife, being very uneasy at the liberties the gentlemen took in looking on and talking to her, solicited Don Medenta to procure him some little seat in the country, and had it forthwith granted; for the governor sent him to a little market-town about twenty miles from the city, to a house of pleasure which he had there; and here he found a little paradise, a house so neat and richly furnished, such lovely gardens, fish-ponds, fountains, fields and groves, that his imagination could not have formed a more beautiful retreat. Having viewed it, and got all things ready, that is, two servants, and the rooms aired, he came back to the castle to fetch his wife, and return thanks for his fine being. But when Ifabinda took leave of Charlotta, they both wept, and Charlotta promised to go every summer and pass her time there. Here Domingo and his little family lived happily the remainder of their days, having many children, and Ifabinda by his persuasions became a true Roman Catholic. But Charlotta continued some time a Protestant in her heart; yet at last she was truly happy in her own thoughts, and pleased she was Don Medenta's wife; for she had all that mortal could wish for, a noble fortune, lovely children, and a husband who loved her beyond expression, and denied her nothing.

And now we must mention the pirate-captain, who was safely landed on this island, and cured of his wounds; the pirate-ship which Gonzalo had taken and sent away before, with the pirates he had taken aboard of it, being arrived at St. Domingo before Gonzalo's ship: This gentleman, who was kept a prisoner in the town, hearing of Don Medenta's marriage with Charlotta, sent her a letter to ask her pardon for what was past, protesting he was truly penitent, and that he honored her virtue as much as he had loved her person; and begged she would procure his enlargement from that dismal place. This letter she showed not her lord; but without relating what had pass'd between her and the pirate, spoke in his behalf; and told him, that he was a Catholick, and a man nobly born, and forced against his will to become a pirate, and that she begged the favor of him to release him, and some way provide for him in the fleet or garrison. This Don Medenta readily granted; and after speaking to his father, went to the prison and released him and two other gentlemen whom he pleaded for, saying they were his countrymen and friends, and not guilty of any crimes but what they had been forced to. The common sailors of the pirates were ordered on board the Spanish galleons, and these three gentlemen followed their benefactor to the castle, to return their thanks to the governor, Don Medenta presenting them to his wife and father. Charlotta looked on the pirate-captain with some disorder; but he addressed himself to her in these terms, making a profound bow, "Madam, I am doubly indebted to you both for my liberty and reformation; I am by your reproofs and generosity freed from both the means and inclinations to sin, and now resolve to live so, that my actions may witness my love to God, and gratitude to you. I will henceforth endeavor to be an honor to my country and religion." This speech much pleased her, who perfectly understood his meaning. And in a short time after, the governor gave him a commission of a captain who died in the garrison, and he married a merchant's widow in the town, who brought him a great fortune. His two companions, according to the custom of the Irish, made their fortunes there also, and settled in that island.

And now we must return to the unfortunate Belanger, whom we left at Virginia much indisposed, which prevented him from coming to the Island of St. Domingo for some time. Monsieur du Pont being highly caressed by Don Medenta and all his friends, as being Charlotta's near kinsman, soon obtained money and a ship to go to Canada in search of Angelina, promising to stop at that island in his return, before he went home to France.

CHAPTER 12

Monsieur Belanger, after ten months' sickness, employed his kinsman Lewis de Montandre to hire a bark secretly to carry them to the island of St. Domingo, fearing Madam de Santerell should get knowledge of his design, and again follow him; besides, he knew her passion would be so violent, that he should scarce be able to leave her. She was now in a deep consumption, and had been so kind to him, that he was obliged to withdraw himself with great reluctance; and had he known Charlotta was disposed of, no doubt but he would have married this unfortunate lady, who now dearly paid for her parting him from her rival; for she had like to have died with grief after he left her. His kinsman got a bark, and acquainted his father with their design; who, to forward it, having nothing to object against it, since Belanger and the lady were contracted, as he assured him they were, took Madam de Santerell with him to a lady's who was related to him, and had a fine plantation not far from his, persuading her it would be good for her health to stay there a few days. Belanger promised to fetch her home soon, and taking leave of her, found himself in so great disorder, that he was like to swoon, conscious that he designed to flee her no more; and stung with a sense of his ingratitude to her, who so passionately loved him, he was in the utmost disorder. She likewise, as if apprehensive of her misfortune, let fall a shower of tears: thus parted, never to meet again, as he supposed. He went aboard with his kinsman, and set sail for the island, where he was to meet with greater misfortunes than he ever yet met with.

So soon as the ship was gone off the coast, Monsieur de Montandre, Belanger's uncle, who was a widower, and was fallen in love with Madam de Santerell, glad of this opportunity (as he hoped) to cure her of her passion for his nephew, rode over to his kinswoman's, where he had two days before left her, to acquaint her with his being gone, aggravating the baseness of his leaving her thus treacherously, and vile ingratitude to her. But she, as one thunder-struck, made little reply; but casting up her eyes to Heaven, with a deep sigh cried, "'Tis just, my God, I am the criminal, and he is innocent; affection cannot be forced: I vainly strove against thy decrees, and ask no more but to be forgiven, and to die." She fainted away, and was carried to her chamber, where the lady of the house endeavored all she was able to comfort her. And to her she related all her story, not concealing the subtle stratagem she had made use of to get Belanger from her rival, saying, "'Tis but just that I should suffer for my crime and folly in persevering to love him, who cannot return it as he ought." She so abandoned herself to these sad thoughts, that her sickness daily increased, and they despaired of her continuing long alive. She was very sensible of her own condition, and seemed much pleased with the thoughts of death; for besides the loss of the man she so excessively loved, the sense she had of her own folly, and the desperateness of her circumstances, being left in a stranger's care, (with whom indeed Belanger had left money to provide for, and carry her home to France; but thither she was ashamed to return; besides, it might be long ere her health would permit her to take such a voyage) All these sad reflections overwhelmed her, and had doubtless killed her, had not Providence mercifully prolonged her life to be happy.

Monsieur Montandre showed the greatest concern and affection for her that a man could possibly make appear; professing he desired no greater happiness on earth than the continuance of her life, and would give all his fortune to save her. All the physicians of note in the place were made use of, and at last, art and nature joined together, raised her from her sick bed; and then reason took place over fancy, and she hearkened to Montandre's proposal, whose generosity put in the balance with Belanger's ingratitude, and the impossibility of her being his, prevailed with her to accept of his offer. Thus she was happily provided for, and Belanger lost a great part of his uncle's fortune which he had designed to give him, never designing to marry again, till he saw this young lady, by whom he had many fine children to inherit what he could settle on them (without injuring his eldest son) which was very considerable.

In few days after his departure, Belanger arrived safely with his kinsman at the island of St. Domingo; and being a stranger there, got the captain of the bark, who was used to trade there, to take them a lodging, thinking it most prudent not to appear too openly in a place where his rival's father was governor, till he had got information how Charlotta was disposed of; which he soon learned to his inexpressible grief. His kinsman making inquiry after her of Gonzalo, the captain of the ship that brought her thither, whom he met with at a coffee-house to which he was directed; he told him of her marriage and good fortune, as he termed it. And indeed so it was, had her lover never come to ruin her peace.

Belanger was quite distracted with this news; his kinsman wisely advised him to return to Virginia, and never see her. "She cannot be blamed," said he, "she was left in your rival's power, and has wisely chosen rather to marry, and be his wife with honour, than to be his mistress by compulsion, and be ruined; and now it would be cruel and ungenerous to revive her grief by seeing her. Besides, should her husband be informed of your speaking to her, it might make her miserable all the rest of her days; and this would be an ill proof of your love to her." This, and a thousand things more, he said to persuade him to be gone; but all to no purpose: he was deaf as the winds, and behaved himself like a madman. At last he resolved to go to the church she used on festival-days, disguised in a Spanish habit, which the captain of the bark procured him, and have a sight of her, promising not to attempt to speak to her.

It was the cathedral-church; and the Sunday following, Belanger, who had not stirred out of his lodging from the day of his arrival, which was on the Wednesday before, went with his kinsman to the high-mass, where he saw the charming Charlotta, who was great with child, standing by her husband and father-in-law next the altar, and the lovely Teresa by her, four crimson velvet chairs being placed within the rails on a rich carpet for them. She was dressed in a Spanish dress, rich as art could make it, and had a store of jewels in her hair and on her breast; thus adorned, he thought her more beautiful than ever, and felt such tortures in his soul, that he could not govern his passion, but dropped down in a swoon, which occasioned some disorder among the people. The crowd was so great, that he could not be carried out, but was unfortunately brought near the rails. Charlotta turning her head, soon knew his face, gave a great shriek, and swooned, falling back into one of the chairs. Don Medenta's jealousy was presently awakened, and he too truly guessed who was in the church; but Belanger's kinsman prudently fearing a discovery, got him carried out into the air, and muffling his face up in his cloak, led him home to their lodging, being come to himself so soon as he came into the open air. Charlotta's fainting was supposed to be occasioned by her being surprised at the noise in the church, or with heat, being with child; this passed with all but her Lord, who upon her recovering, led her to his coach, and went home with her, being impatient to question her what she saw that so much disordered her. She said she thought the Spaniard that fainted was so like Belanger, that being surprised, she could not but be so discomposed. He desired her to go no more into public assemblies till she was up again, resolving in himself to set such spies at work, that if Belanger was arrived there, he should soon be sent farther off, or dispatched. She promised to do whatever he would have her, and he seemed contented. But his soul was so inflamed with jealousy, that he could rest no more till he was satisfied of the truth, and had secured his rival.

It was not many hours before those he set at work to discover who this person was that had occasioned this disorder in the church, informed him that two gentlemen were arrived in a ship from Virginia, and lodged privately in the town; that one of them made inquiry after Charlotta, meeting Gonzalo at the coffee-house. In fine, his suspicions were now confirmed, and he persuaded Charlotta to go to Domingo's in the country, to pass a month with Isabinda, saying it would be better for her to be in a place where she would be freed from receiving ceremonious visits, and could better indulge herself in that sweet retirement; and that she should continue there till she was near her time, if she pleased.

She willingly consented, being now deeply melancholy, and glad of an opportunity to be alone with her dear friend Isabinda, to whom she could unbosom her thoughts. He carried her thither, and left her, pretending he had business that obliged him to return to his father; concluding in his own thoughts that Belanger, who no doubt was impatient to speak with her, would soon learn where she was, follow her, and venture to pay her a visit, she being absent. The old lady or governess, who attended her, was his creature, and he left her a spy on all her actions. He took his leave as usual, with all the tenderness imaginable, saying he should think each day a year till he returned to her.

All things were transacted as he foresaw. Belanger, learning he was absent, and Charlotta at the country-house, went with his friend disguised in their Spanish dresses, to the village where she was, and took a lodging in a peasant's house, where they kept very private for two days. Then his friend Montandre, who ventured abroad for intelligence, being certain that he was not known by Don Medenta, having seen her walking in the gardens with Isabinda, informed him of it; so they consulted what to do. And Belanger, fearing to surprise her a second time, resolved to write a letter to her, and send it by his friend. The contents of which were as follow:

Still charming though perjured Charlotta,

After a tedious sickness, occasioned by my grief for the loss of you, which long confined me to my bed, and brought me almost to the grave, I am come to this island, where I have learned the cruel news that you are now another's. I shall make you no reproaches, nor ask anything but the honour of one hour's conversation with you, after which you shall never more be importuned or disordered with the sight of me. I love you as passionately as ever, and only desire to prove it by dying at your feet. Let it be soon, lest grief deprive me of that satisfaction; for my soul is so transported with despair, that only the hope of seeing you once more, keeps me alive. My angel, name the place and time to my friend, and for the last time oblige.

Your constant undone,
Belanger.

THIS LETTER WAS DELIVERED into Charlotta's hand by Montandre the next morning; for he ventured to go into the gardens before day over the stone wall, and there hid himself in a summer-house till Charlotta came into the garden to walk with her friend Isabinda alone. He took this, as he thought, lucky opportunity, and at their coming into the summer-house to sit down, presented himself and the letter to her. She was a little startled, but believing Belanger was not gone from the island, she expected to hear from or see him, concluding he would by some means or other find a way to send or come to her; so she immediately guessed who he came from.

She read the moving lines, and shedding a flood of tears, said, "Sir, tell the unfortunate Belanger it was his misfortune, not my fault, that we are separated; his leaving me put me under a fatal necessity of giving myself to him in whose power I was left. I am now disposed of to a noble husband, whom I am bound to love and honour. It is altogether improper for me to admit of a visit from the man whom I have loved, and still have too much inclination for. Besides, it is inconsistent with my honour, and may be both our ruin. I make it my last request to him therefore to leave this island immediately, and conjure him, as he values his own life, or my peace, not to attempt seeing me, or to stay here a day longer. My husband is already alarmed, and has, I fear, brought me to this place with design to betray him. For Heaven's sake persuade him to fly hence, and not render me entirely miserable. Tell him, I beg him to remember me no more, but in his prayers, and to submit with a Christian resignation to the will of Heaven. This is all I can say to him, and my final answer."

At these words she rose, and went out of the summer-house, leaving Isabinda to let him out at the back gate with a key which she always carried in her pocket, to let them into a grove which was behind the garden. Isabinda hastened him away, entreating him never to return. Charlotta retired to her closet, and there gave way to her passion; her love to Belanger was now revived, and she had the most dreadful apprehensions of his danger that can be conceived. She perused the dear lines he had sent her a hundred times over, and washed them pale with her tears. Whilst she was thus employed, Don Medenta, who had lain all the time in the village, and had received information of the strangers lodging at the peasant's, and of Montandre's being in the garden (Charlotta having been watched by the old duenna), knocked at the closet-door. She asked who was there; and hearing his voice, clapped the letter into her bosom, and opened the door in such a disorder that her lord would have been much surprised at, if he had not known the cause of it before. He took her in his arms with a forced air of affection, but his eyes flashed with rage; he trembled, and spoke in so distracted a manner, that she too well perceived he was informed of what had passed, and was so overcome with grief, that she fainted in his arms. He laid her gently on the couch, and took the letter out of her bosom, read it, and putting it there again, called the old governess who waited without, and presently fetched cordials to bring her to herself; but they tried all means in vain so long, that he thought her dead, and indeed began to abandon himself to passion.

Isabinda, who had retired to her chamber, seeing Don Medenta go into the apartment as she was going to give Charlotta an account that the gentleman was gone away in safety, hearing his complaints, came in, and also thought her dead. The physicians were called, and by their aid she was brought to life, but immediately fell in labour, being seven months gone with child. This caused a great deal of confusion in the family, where nothing was prepared for her lying-in, it being designed to be in the castle with the utmost magnificence. At three in the afternoon she was delivered of a son, who lived but a few hours, and was therefore by the physicians' advice baptized as soon as it was born. Don Medenta was highly afflicted at his own imprudence in surprising her, and showed the utmost tenderness and concern for her, kneeling by her bed-side on the floor, kissing her hands, professing that he loved and valued her above all earthly things, and could not live without her; till at last the physicians entreated him to quit the room, and leave her to repose. So the chamber being darkened, and none but nurses left to attend her, poor Charlotta was delivered up to her own sad thoughts, which soon threw her into a fever which had like to have ended her life.

And now Don Medenta was ten times more enraged against Belanger than before, looking upon him as the cause of his child's death, and perhaps of his beloved Charlotta's, for which he now resolved to be revenged of him. In order to this, he immediately set four bravoes, whom he had before hired, and placed ready to seize him, to watch his lodgings. They were all disguised, and hid themselves in a field behind the peasant's house. Towards the dusk of the evening they perceived Belanger and his friend go forth, and take the way to Domingo's; they followed, and so soon as they saw them enter the grove, seized them. Montandre had dissuaded him from this attempt all he was able, but he was determined to see Charlotta or die; and since his friend had so easily got the speech of her, flattered himself he should have the same good fortune; but when he found himself seized by villains, gagged and bound, with his generous friend, who was like to be made a sacrifice for his folly, he bitterly repented his rashness. They were thrown across a horse like calves, their legs and hands being fastened with a cord under the horse's belly, a sumpter-horse-cloth was thrown over them, and thus they were carried all night, guarded by the four bravoes, who were well armed, and had a pass from the governor's son, so that none offered to stop them.

By break of day they arrived at an old castle, well fortified, on the north side of the island, where an officer and twelve soldiers were in garrison, who had received orders before what to do with these unfortunate gentlemen, whom he was to keep secure in the castle-dungeon, being pirates, desperate villains, and reserved to make discoveries, by the rack, if they would not do it voluntarily. Don Medenta confirmed all this to the officer by a letter he sent him some days before. Into the dungeon they were accordingly carried, put in irons, and left to live upon the allowance the officer was ordered to give them, which was very sufficient: for Don Medenta was not willing to load his conscience with the guilt of murdering them, but only desired to secure his own repose and his wife's honour, and would willingly have sent them to any place, and set them at liberty, could he but have been secured from their ever returning to St. Domingo. To Belanger's friend he had no prejudice; nay, he rather had an esteem for him, for the generous friendship he had shown in risking his life for his friend.

These gentlemen thus secured, the bravoes went back to Don Medenta, who on this news was more at ease, and applied his whole thoughts about Charlotta's indisposition. She was many days light-headed, calling often upon Belanger, which stabbed him to the heart. It was more than six months before she was able to go out of her chamber. In this time she often asked Isabinda if she could tell any news of Belanger, and was much troubled that she could hear nothing of him. Sometimes she flattered herself that he had prudently taken her advice, and left the island; yet inwardly reproached him with want of affection. Then reflecting on his daring temper and constancy, which his venturing thither after her did evidence, she concluded he had heard of her illness, and lay still concealed there. Then she trembled with the thoughts of his being discovered, or ruining himself and her by venturing to speak to her; another while she feared he was murdered. So soon as she was able, Don Medenta carried her to the castle, where his father received her with much joy, and all the ladies paid her visits, congratulating her recovery. The ship that brought Belanger set sail, having waited two months, and returned to Virginia, at which his uncle and Madam de Santerell were much surprised, but concluded that he was gone home to France; and they were much concerned at young Montandre's not returning or writing; but were fain to rest satisfied, expecting to hear from them.

CHAPTER 13

When the wretched Belanger saw himself and his friend in this dismal place, no words can express the tortures of his mind; and indeed it was a providence he was at that time fettered, or else his despair might have driven him to destroy himself. He sighed deeply, and the big drops ran scalding down his cheeks; grief had so benumbed his faculties, that his tongue could not utter one word; so that he remained silent, with his eyes fixed on his friend, who bore his afflictions calmly; for he had not love and despair to combat, had lost no mistress, loved his friend, and had a soul so generous, that he was even glad, since it was his fate to be thus confined, that he was a partner of his fortune, and reserved to comfort him in that sad place.

"Why," said he to the afflicted Belanger, "my dear friend, do you thus abandon yourself to grief, and are so cast down at an accidental misfortune? Could you expect less than this from an incensed husband? Is it not a mercy you are still alive? When we went from our lodgings, we were determined to run all risks, and are you shocked at a thing you had before armed against? Your jealous rival's rage will in time diminish; and when he comes to reflect on this action, he will doubtless repent, and permit you to depart this island. If he persists in his revenge, death is the utmost we can fear; and can there be a place more fit to prepare for it than this? Here we may live free from the temptations of the world, and learn the state of our own souls; nay, converse with our maker by contemplation, and enjoy that peace of mind, that we were strangers to whilst we lived at large. Consider how many brave men have perished for want abroad, and how many pious persons have retreated to dismal caves and deserts, and left all the delights of this life, to enjoy that quiet and repose which we may here possess. Charlotta has already, doubtless, suffered for your imprudence; and in pursuing her, you offended Heaven, who having thus punished you, on your submission will (I doubt not) free you hence. As for my own part, I am so far from repenting I accompanied you, that I rejoice that God has been pleased to preserve me, and bring me to this place to comfort you; nor would I leave you, though I were freed."

Belanger having been very attentive to all he said, replied: "Was ever generosity like this? What a miserable wretch am I, that by my follies have ruined the peace of her I loved, and subjected my faithful generous friend to fetters and a dungeon? I merit all that I can suffer; but your presence puts me on the rack, yet I will hope. My God, thy ways are marvelous; in thee I'll trust, and strive to bring my stubborn will to submit to thine."

The first transports of his passion being thus conquered, he began to be resigned. And now food and wine being brought to them, they eat thankfully what was provided, and for some days conversed and prayed together, like men prepared for all events; but the damp unwholesome vapors in the dungeon threw them both into an illness, taking away the use of their limbs, that the commanding officer, who was a French man, sent to Don Medenta, to know what he should do with them; assuring him they would die, if not soon removed. On which he sent orders to him, to remove them to an apartment on the top of the castle, where they might walk on the battlements and take the air, have a bed, and chambers to walk about, and their fetters taken off. His conscience touched him, and he would willingly have freed Montandre, but that he feared he would make a clamor about his friend.

These orders were punctually obeyed by the officer, and the prisoners soon recovered. And he sometimes paid them a visit, and so became informed of the true cause of their being brought thither, and pitied their condition. At last he contracted so great a friendship with them, that he said he would willingly free them, could he be assured he should not lose his commission by it. But it would not be long, he supposed, before he should be relieved by another officer and band of soldiers, it being customary for the garrison to be changed every six months; and then he would furnish them with ropes to let themselves down from the battle-ments, on that side of the castle next the sea, which beat against the walls; and that they need not fear drowning, the water being shallow at ebb.

"Thence," says he, "you may get to the shore, and disguised in two soldiers' coats, which I will give you; hide yourselves in the adjacent wood. This you must do in the night, and get off the island, if possible, as soon as day breaks, for fear of being taken; for search will doubtless be made for you so soon as you are missed. You may effect this by seizing the first fishing-boat you find on the shore, of which there are many, plenty of huts being in these parts on the coast, where fish-ermen dwell during this summer-season; and you will find their boats, which are every night hauled up on the shore. This is all I dare do to serve you, and this perhaps will cost me my life, if discovered."

They not only thanked him in the most expressive terms, but promised if they ever lived to reach Virginia again, to show their grat-itude. And he promised to give them intelligence of whatever befell Charlotta, by the captain who brought them thither, whom they resolved to send to that island yearly, he giving them a direction where they should always inquire for him. This concluded on, Belanger and Montandre grew cheerful.

At last orders coming for the officer to depart thence, he faithfully performed all he had promised, leaving them ropes and red coats; nay, when he took his leave, which he did with much affection, he presented Belanger with a good purse of gold, which he had much ado to make him accept of. But indeed it was necessary they should not want money, of which they had no great store about them, having left all their clothes and money at the lodging in which the captain of the ship had placed them at their landing in the town; for they brought nothing to the peasant's house in the village, but some linen and about twenty pistoles in gold, and some Spanish ducatoons in silver, in their pockets.

The very night after the captain was gone they made their escape, Montandre venturing down first from the battlements, having sworn his friend should not venture till he had tried the danger; for it was a vast height from whence they descended, and had the rope broken, he had run a great risk of losing his life. They fastened two ropes to the top of one of the battlements, and putting their gloves on, slid down one after the other into the sea, which then was so high, it being young flood, that it almost took them up to their breasts, and the waves beat so strong, that they had much ado to reach the shore; from whence they fled to the wood, and passed through it to the other side. There sheltered by the trees from the view of the garrison, they stood a while to see what boats lay on the shore; and choosing such a one as they thought they were able to manage, and launch into the sea without help, they dragged it into the water, and getting into it, hoisted sail, and put off.

But alas! their condition was worse than ever, they knew not well how to steer the boat, and were so weak and tired before, that they could scarce row or guide it. They had no provisions aboard but a little biscuit and salt meat, that they found stowed in the fisherman's locker in his cabin, with a bottle of rack, and a small barrel of fresh water. And now all their hopes were to reach some island not belonging to the Spaniards; they steered for Jamaica, from whence they were certain they could get a passage to Virginia, where Belanger resolved to remain with his uncle and friend till Charlotta was dead, or a widow; and never return to France again without her, whilst she was living.

They were in sight of Jamaica, when the wind began to blow and the waters foam: then a terrible storm began, which drove them for four nights and days quite out of their knowledge; in which time their provisions were spent, and their strength so decayed, that they were forced to lie down, and leave themselves to providence. But nothing afflicted them so much as thirst; all their fresh water was gone, and drinking salt, increased their drought, that they feared to repeat it. Thus they continued for three days more driven by the winds and waves. In these three days hunger so pressed them, that they ransacked every corner of the boat to find a morsel to eat, and devoured every bit of moldy biscuit they could find: but alas! that was so little, it only tantalized, not satisfied their craving stomachs. And now they began to reflect, that it had been better for them to have continued prisoners, than have exposed themselves to such miseries. Thus experience tells us, that when we have obtained our own wishes, not easy in the state providence has placed us in, we are more unhappy than we were before.

And now the generous Montandre begged his kinsman to kill him, and preserve his own life, by feeding on his warm flesh, and sucking his blood, saying, "We must now both inevitably perish, unless one supply the other's wants." Belanger was so shocked at this proposal, that his very soul shivered. "No," says he, "before I would destroy you, I would eat my own flesh: No, we will live and die together: We have this night passed over many banks of sand, and are doubtless near some shore; now pluck up your spirit, and let us redouble our importunity to God to send us a deliverance."

Before the words were out of his mouth a wave tossed a large dolphin into the boat, which they killed with the oars, and fell to eating, sucking the warm blood and raw flesh more greedily than ever they had done the most delicious food prepared for them. This greatly refreshed them, and towards sun-setting the wind abating, they laid by their oars, and fell to eating more of the raw fish, but sparingly, not knowing how long they had to live upon it. Whilst they were at this strange supper they spied land, on which they applied themselves a fresh to their oars, and about midnight reached the shore; but not knowing where they were, dragged the boat up on the sand, and lay in it till day-break, having been driven in by the tide with such violence, that they could not stop her before she struck on the sands.

When day appeared they found they had entered into the Gulf of Mexico, between the isles of Cuba and Incatan, and were landed on that coast where the Spaniards were masters. They thought it best to pretend they were Frenchmen, who, being cast away in a ship, had escaped death by getting into that fishing-boat, which the wind had (as they supposed) driven out to sea from the Havana, near which they pretended the ship they were in perished; for though they had soldiers' coats on, yet their Spanish habits showed they were gentlemen, and their behavior showed their breeding. The Spaniards received them kindly, and a merchant took them into his house, where he entertained them very generously, and invited them to continue there till they could find means to go to Virginia, telling them it was their best way to do so by some trading vessel, which he supposed they must wait some time for. This merchant had a bark ready to sail with goods for Carolina, from whence it would not be very difficult for them to go by land to Virginia. He offered them a passage in this ship, which they gladly accepted of; and in few days went aboard, and got safe to Carolina. They hired a guide to conduct them through the country to Virginia; but passing by the Apalatean Mountains, a party of Indians came down upon them, and carrying them away over the mountains, plundered them of their money and clothes.

Amongst these Indians they continued four whole years in the greatest misery, being obliged to live after their barbarous fashion as slaves; till going out with a party to cut fuel in the thick woods, they took their opportunity to make their escape, being desperate, and hid themselves in a cave in the night, choosing rather to venture being devoured by wild beasts, than spend their lives in slavery. They lay concealed in this place till the Indians were gone farther on; and then, destitute of food, and in their slaves' dress, they fled towards one of the Spanish forts, which they could never have reached had they not met with an old hermit, who lived in a poor cottage near a wood. He was standing at his door, and seeing two poor slaves, who looked like death, come towards him, supposed they were in want and Christians, so invited them in, to their great surprise, and gave them bread and drink, asking where they were going. They gave him this account, that they were cast away in a ship, saved in a fishing-boat near the Havana, driven on the coast of Incatan; from thence went in a bark to Carolina, and going across the countries for Virginia, were taken and made slaves; and wearied with the miseries they endured, were now endeavoring to escape to Fort-Philip. He told them, he would conduct them thither in safety the next morning. They stayed with him all night, lying on straw (as he did) with warm coverlets: And being very importunate to know the reasons of his living this solitary life, he told them his story in these words.

CHAPTER 14

I am, said he, by birth a Frenchman; I was the younger son of a counsellor, who had a great estate, and was put in a good post under my father so soon as I was able to understand business, having a clerk's place in the Salt-Office. Here being from under my father's eye, I contracted an intimacy with a young gentlewoman who lived with her aunt, a person who, though well-born, was fallen to decay, and they maintained themselves by their needles, and some small income the aunt had left, very genteelly, but with much diffi-culty. It was my fortune to see this young woman at church, she was very beautiful and genteel. I followed her home, made love to her, and was well received. I pretended an honorable affection; but, alas, had no other design in my wicked heart but to debauch her.

Their circumstances made them willingly receive the presents and treats I gave them, not thinking it dishonorable, since I pretended marriage; glad was the innocent creature to be so provided for. Their conversation was charming, and their conduct so reserved and modest, that I was a great while before I could venture to make any attempt upon her virtue; but then I was repulsed with such scorn and reproofs, that I almost despaired of effecting my base design. But knowing that it would be my ruin if I married her, and being now so much in love, that I knew not how to live without her, I still persisted in my visits and importunities, and though refused the sight of her frequently, and always received with reproaches, yet I could not desist; and finding all my attempts were in vain, and that I could not reduce her to my will, at last I consented to marry her privately, on condition that she should keep it a secret. This she gladly consented to, and so we were married by a Cordelier who was her confessor: and then I was made happy in the possession of my dear Louisa, who was the most virtuous and most charming woman breathing.

Here he shed some tears, and could scarce go on; but recovering, he continued his discourse thus: And now, gentlemen, I am going to relate a part of my life, that fills my soul with horror, and will, I hope, deter all that hear it from committing such crimes. We passed some months as happily as we could wish, and she grew great with child; but my expenses increasing, and a prospect of more charges coming on, made me grow something uneasy; to add to which, my father began to press me about a marriage that was proposed to him much to my advantage. This put anxious thoughts into my head, and made me reflect how imprudent I had been. My eager desires were satisfied, my love diminished, as my ambition and avarice were increased; and in fine, I wished her dead, and meditated on nothing but how to get rid of her.

Thus my disobedience in marrying without my father's knowledge and consent, drew down Heaven's anger upon me, and the devil tempted me on to proceed to more flagrant crimes. I did not visit my wife so often as usual, but humored my father in visiting the young lady proposed to me, who was every way agreeable, and had the most prevailing argument on her side to engage man's inconstant heart, that is, a great fortune: she was the only daughter of a rich banker, had taken a fancy to me, and her parents doating on her, resolved not to cross her, for which reason they made the proposal to my father. Such advances were made on their side, that I could find no pretense to delay the marriage longer. And now I foresaw that I must either incur my father's hatred, and be ruined, (for he was a man of an implacable temper, and would, I knew, abandon me, if he discovered my marriage) or else that I must rid myself of Louisa forthwith, and then I might be great, and, as I vainly flattered myself, happy.

This wicked thought I indulged, and long resolved in my mind, till at last, I resolved to put it in execution; and though I was grievously tormented in my conscience, yet I persevered in this wicked design, and bought poison, which I made an infusion of in wine, and putting it into a vial in my pocket, I went to my virtuous wife to lie all night. She received me with open arms; I appeared more cheerful and kind than usual; we supped, and after supper I pretended I was not well, and desired we might have some burnt wine, which her aunt presently got. I slyly poured the poison into the cup, which I presented to my dear wife, pretending she and her aunt must drink with me; they readily complied, always studying to oblige me. But when I saw Louisa swallow it, my soul shivered, my conscience flew in my face; and when she came and kissed me as I was going to bed, I felt tortures not to be expressed, or indeed conceived, but by such wretches as myself.

She had not lain long in my arms, but convulsions seized her nerves, and I called her aunt and servant up, showing the greatest concern; but neither of them suspected what was the matter, nor need I counterfeit, for at that instant I was filled with such horrors, that I would have given the whole world to save her. From this moment my peace was broken, and I became the most miserable man breathing. She expired in my arms before day, with the dear murdered infant in her; saying the kindest things to me and praying for me even in the last agonies of death. The innocent Louisa thus dispatched, I took leave, giving money to her aunt (who was almost distracted with grief) to bury her. They had kept a maid-servant ever since my marriage, and I left them in the house, and excused myself from being present at her burial, lest my father should hear of it; promising the aunt to be always kind to her.

Having left these melancholy objects, I went to the tavern, drank a quart of wine to revive my spirits, and then went home to my father's. And now my whole business was to divert my thoughts as much as possible; I went abroad every day, drank, danced, went to the play, and so lulled myself with variety of pleasures, that the terrors of my conscience were something silenced. The sad impressions of Louisa's murder wore off, and I was married; but the bridal-night I was no sooner in bed, and the candles extinguished, than as I was going to take my bride in my arms, the curtain at my bed's-head was drawn back, and turning my head, I saw Louisa standing by my side, big with child, and the fatal vial in her hand, which she seemed to shake, and looked upon me with a look that struck quite through my soul; the cold sweat trickled down my face, and the bed shook under me, every nerve shivered, as if the agonies of death had seized me.

Thus I lay, with my eyes shut, not daring to lift up my eye-lids, till the day-break had freed me from this dreadful vision, which made such an impression on my soul, that I fancied her ever in my sight, and could not relish nor take any satisfaction in any thing I possessed. I concealed this from the world, and did all that was possible to oblige my new wife, who was doatingly fond of me, and had brought me a great a fortune, that we wanted nothing that wealth could purchase, to make us happy in a moderate way of life. But wealth could not cure my wounded conscience; I had a load of guilt upon my soul, and was continually upon the rack; this soon destroyed my health, and so afflicted her, that she was almost as unhappy as myself.

Being through weakness, attended with an intermitting fever, confined to my bed, I seriously prepared for death, and confessed myself to a Franciscan, a man of great wisdom and piety, who so eloquently laid before me the enormity of my crime, the terrors of eternal punishment, and the infinite mercies of God on a sincere repentance, that I heartily lamented my sins, and endeavored to reconcile myself to God; on which he was pleased to raise me up again, and prolong my life. My wife was now great with child, and had never had the smallpox, which she unfortunately caught by going to an opera, where she saw a person newly recovered, and at her coming home was taken ill, and died of them.

Being now left a widower, the thoughts I had in my late sickness, came afresh into my mind, and I resolved to retire from the world; but my father and friends much opposed it, being desirous I should marry again, because my elder brother was consumptive, and though married seven years, had no child. The prospect of having all my father's fortune prevailed with me not to enter into the church into any religious community; but being still uneasy in my mind, thinking I ought to do something to atone for my sins, I resolved to retire to some remote part of the world to do penance for them by fasting, and prayers, and alms-deeds. I therefore put all my estate into my confessor's hands, to distribute the income of it every year to the poor, and return me forty pounds a year to this place by the hands of a gentleman who is an officer in Fort-Philip, to which you are designed to go: with him I came to this part of the world, being my intimate friend and near relation. He receives my income, and when I want provisions or money, I repair to him.

My poverty and manner of living, makes the Indians never molest me, nay they love me, and supply me with any thing I want: Besides I am a kind of physician amongst them; for having taken delight in studying physic, I am arrived to some knowledge in it, and well acquainted with the nature and use of all the medicinal herbs that grow in these parts. I am also part of a surgeon, and dress their wounds and sores, and by this means have many opportunities of saving their bodies and souls, by instructing them in the Christian faith. I speak their languages, and often procure the freedom of those Christians, who like you have unfortunately fallen into their hands. Thus I have lived for these eight years, and am now so inured to this solitary way of living, and so satisfied with this poor retreat, that I do not think ever to return to France again, or venture into the world any more; and hoping I have made my peace with God, I wait my death as a man who places his hopes on an eternal state.

Thus he concluded his story. Belanger, who during this discourse was filled with admiration, yet never interrupted him, now broke silence: "Monsieur du Riviere," said he, "what transport can equal mine to find you here? I have news to tell you will recall you soon to France. I shall tell you wonders."

"Is not your name Belanger," said the amazed hermit, "and have I the happiness to meet with and entertain the youth whom I so dearly loved?"

"Yes," said Belanger, "I am that man whom you were pleased to honor with your friendship in so peculiar a manner; and to convince you that the Almighty has accepted your repentance and alms-deeds, am doubtless sent to this place to set your mind at ease, and restore that peace of conscience that you have been so long a stranger to. Louisa is, I hope, still living; she was in perfect health six years ago when I left France."

"Louisa living!" said the hermit, "amazing wonder! my ravished soul can scarce credit the strange report, though from my best loved friend. Speak, tell me the manner how she was preserved from death, whilst my listening wounded soul is healed with the soft sound of your sweet speech."

"I will make haste," said Belanger, "to satisfy you. So soon as you had left the house, Louisa's aunt, who had been before informed of all your actions, knew your courtship to your new mistress, and frequent visits there, had marked your coldness to and neglect of Louisa, and made observations on your behavior that fatal night, and her sudden illness and surprising death; the minute you turned your back, ran to the convent, which you know was not a stone's throw from the house, and called up the honest Cordelier, who had married you, a man who was a good physician as well as a divine, and told him with tears the strange manner of Louisa's death, which he immediately suspected to be the effect of poison; and taking some strong emetics with him, ran to the house as fast as his legs could carry him, and finding her body warm and pliant, poured enough down her throat to effect his good design; for it so wrought, that it soon brought up the baneful drug, and with more proper applications, at last restored her oppressed faculties to their use, and her to life and health, with the innocent child, so that both were preserved, and she perfectly recovered in a few days; which they kept a secret by his advice."

"Since your cruel husband," said he, "has this time failed of executing his wicked purpose, he will no doubt repeat the attempt, and may at last succeed; to avoid which, you shall retire to a convent of our order, where my sister is abbess, there care shall be taken of you and the child. Let him suffer the remorse of his own conscience, and smart for his sin, nor be freed from his torments by knowing you are saved. When he dies, I will do justice to the child if it lives, and seize the estate. Mean time you shall know how he fares with his new choice, and be freed from those fears which his knowledge of your being alive will subject you to." She consented, and has continued in this convent ever since, with her son, who was born there. All this I was informed of by her aunt, my near kinswoman, who had made me privy to your marriage, and engaged me not to disclose it; but now it ought to be no longer a secret to you, since you are truly penitent.

The hermit fell on his knees, and with a flood of tears returned thanks to God, in such moving expressions, as drew tears from Belanger and Montandre's eyes. Then they related the particulars of their adventures; and rising as soon as day appeared, set out together for Fort-Philip, resolving to go to Virginia by the first opportunity, from whence du Riviere might easily get passage to France, being impatient to see and ask pardon of his injured Louisa. Being arrived at Fort-Philip, they were kindly entertained by the hermit's friend, who furnished them with clothes, and a guide, with some soldiers to guard them to Virginia, and protect them from the Indians. This officer being acquainted with his friend's story and Belanger's, gave them money to defray their charges on the way to Virginia, from whence Belanger promised to furnish du Riviere with all necessaries for his return to France.

CHAPTER 15

I am the daughter of a noble Venetian, my brother is a Knight of Malta, my name is Catherina Belmanto de Furnaze. I was placed in a monastery as a pensioner, being but twelve years old; there a young gentleman courted me secretly, the younger son of a noble family, who was a captain in the service of the state, and had no other fortune but his commission, which indeed was sufficient to support him nobly, but was not considerable enough to answer that great fortune my father designed me, or to answer his and my brother's ambitious expectations, I being an only daughter. This gentleman's person and sense gained my affection, so that I preferred him in my heart before all others, gave him my hand and promise to be his; but it was not long ere it was discovered that some conversation had passed between us, and I was sent for home, and questioned, but confessed nothing.

This distracted my lover, and he was impatient at my being kept from him: so that at last he made use of a stratagem to get me, which he thus effected: He sent me a letter by a servant to my father's, which he doubted not would be intercepted; in which he acquainted me, after abundance of passionate assurances, that he would ever love me; that fearing I suffered much contraint and uneasiness on his account, he was resolved to sell his post, and go for Spain, having some great relations there by his mother's side, who was a Spanish lady, by whose interest he doubted not to get a better post; and this was the most generous proof he could give me of his affection, being resolved to make himself miserable to render me happy.

My father, who broke open this letter, was very glad, and had me narrowly watched, till he saw that he did what he pretended, for he sold his post, and took leave of his friends, and went aboard a ship for Spain, as he pretended. Then I was sent back to the monastery, where I soon received a letter from him by means of another pensioner who was our confident; in which he informed me, that he lay concealed at a village hard by, and that he conjured me to get away with the first opportunity, and come to him. This I did the next evening at the close of the day, and got safe to his friend's house where he was concealed. Here he received me with open arms, and his friend's chaplain married us that night. We went away thence before day the next morning, in his coach, which carried us to the port where the ship's boat lay ready to receive us, he having hired the vessel on purpose. We went aboard, weighed anchor, and set sail for Barcelona; but before we could reach that port, we were unfortunately taken by an Algerine pirate, and brought to this dismal place, where I was parted from him, and sold to this vile infidel, to whose cursed bed I have been forced, and have had the misfortune to be liked.

He has been absent these four months, being gone to his country-seat to pass the summer season, where he has other wretched women to divert him; he is to return hither in three days, and then you must be a victim to his lust no question.

Here she let fall a flood of tears, and Angelina bore her company. "You have," said she, "told me a story more unhappy than my own, since I have still preserved my virtue, and am now resolved rather to die than yield, since providence grants me three days for my escape. I'll use that time, and bravely venture to get hence, or die in the attempt; if you will venture with me, speak, I'll lead the way, death is preferable to such a life as this."

"You say you are a Christian, heroic maid," said Catherina, "would you commit self-murder? Is no other way left to free us, or must we kill each other?"

"Far be that dreadful thought," said Angelina, "from my soul; no, I have thought of other means in the short time I have been here. I have observed a Moorish slave whom I saw enter the gardens with a key at a door that leads to the sea, as near as I can guess; that key I am resolved to purchase by his death. Do you contrive some strange disguise to cover us, and pack your jewels up, or what you have of value else, ready to carry out with us, and I will meet him at the gate when he enters at the break of day, as I suppose his custom is, and stab him with a penknife I have hid about me. Could we get the habit of an eunuch for each of us, it would be the safest disguise we could put on; the Bey being absent, and few of his servants left here, and those left on their guard, and more negligent than when he is present, it will not be so difficult to get away as at another time."

"I can procure such habits," said Catherina, "and doubt not, though our apartment is locked up every night, yet the windows are not so high, but we may easily venture down, tying the sheets of our beds together, by which we may slip down into the garden, where in a chamber on one side the seraglio door, two white eunuchs lie to guard it; next this chamber is the wardrobe: if one of us can but get in at the window of this place, and they not hear us, we may have clothes of any kind, and jewels too."

"I will attempt it," said Angelina, "and would prefer all dangers, and even death, to infamy and slavery."

"And so will I," said Catherina.

Being thus resolved, they waited till night came on, when hearing all things still, Angelina crept to her friend's chamber, who had bundled up her jewels and some linen: she got down from the window, and then went to the wardrobe, the moon shining very bright, and were some time before they could contrive how to get in at the window, it being very high; but at last Angelina's wit, which exceeded her sex (though women ever were esteemed more quick and subtle than mankind at cunning plots and quick contrivances) soon found the way to enter; she got on Catherina's shoulders, and went in there trembling; she got two rich vests, two turbans, two pair of Turkish boots, and a box, whose rich outside and weight, though small, made her believe it worth the carrying away; these she bundled up, and threw out of the window to her friend: but then she was at a mighty loss how to get out again, which she in vain attempted, it being impossible for her to get up to the window from whence she had dropped down into the room; no way was left but to pass through the eunuch's chamber, and this necessity prevailed with her to do.

She took down two rich scimitars that hung up in fine embroidered belts, and having drawn one, passed through the chamber where the eunuchs lay fast asleep, resolving if they stirred, to kill them, or to die by their hands. Upon the table there stood a silver bowl half full of wine, of which no doubt they had taken their fill, although their prophet does forbid it them; for few Mussulmen refuse to drink it in private: this bowl she took, with a bunch of keys which lay by it; and going to the door, found the key in it, so she gently unlocked it, and putting it to after her, went out safely to her friend, who stood trembling and almost dead with fear.

Angelina showed her the keys, one of which she fancied would open the garden-gate, to which they hastened, and to their great satisfaction found it so: being got out at the gate, which they locked after them, they stood to consider which way to go, and resolved to get away from the town to the next wood or ruined building they could meet with; they had not gone above two miles, when they entered a grove, at the farther end of which they found an old ruined mosque, which they went into with great fear, lest some old Turkish Brahmin or Santon should live there: but hearing no creature stir but bats and screech-owls, and such vermin as live in unfrequented places, they took courage, and the day beginning to break, they laid down their bundles, and changing their clothes, put on their Turkish habits, which instead of being mean, such as slaves wear, belonged to the Bey himself, being both cloth of gold, the buttons of the one was rubies, and the other emeralds; the turbans were suitably rich, and full of diamonds, pearl, and other jewels: so that they had an immense treasure, had they known how to dispose of it.

But at this time they would willingly have parted with it all for some poor habit to conceal them, fearing they should be pursued and taken, not knowing where to hide themselves: they were weary, faint, and had no food, and searched every corner of this ruinous place to hide themselves; at last they found a door which seemed to lead down some stairs into a vault, where they supposed the dead were buried, and that they should meet with nothing there but skulls and bones and noisome vapors; yet had they had a light, they would gladly have gone into it to hide themselves, nay lived, and chose to sleep and eat amongst the dead, rather than to live luxuriously with infidels. They sat down upon the stairs however to rest their tired limbs; so that if any should pass by, they might shut the door upon them.

As they sat thus consulting what to do, they heard a noise, and saw a man enter the mosque with a dark lantern in his hand and a loaf under his arm, with some scraps of meat, and fish in a little basket; he had a long coarse frize garment on, his face and hands were tawny, he had only sandals on his feet, and a strange fashioned straw-hat upon his head; he sat down his basket and bread, and opening his lantern, turning the light side towards them, came to the door, and was going down stairs, when Catherina giving a great shriek, fell into a swoon upon Angelina, and had like to have beat her down the stairs. It is impossible to express her thoughts at this instant; for though she was a woman of great courage, and had a dauntless soul, yet she was shocked at the instant, as was also the stranger. He looked upon them with amazement; the beauty of their faces, the strange splendor of their habits, and the strange place he found them in, astonished him.

Angelina at last recovering herself, viewed him attentively, and reasoned with herself that he was but a man unarmed, and in all probability as much in distress as themselves; mean time he concluded they were women disguised, and doubtless fled thither for shelter; that they must be Europeans, and persons of birth by their beauty, delicate hands, shape and complexions. He said thus in French to Angelina, "In the name of God what are you, and from whence? Speak, if you understand me, tell me if you are in distress, that I may help you."

"We are by birth Europeans, and profess the Christian Faith," said she, "as I doubt not you do, since you speak my native language; we are fled from ruin, infamy and slavery, and got into this dismal place to screen ourselves from the fury of the infidels whom we this morning fled from. Assist us to escape their hands, and find us means to get hence, and all the riches we have about us shall be yours."

At these words the man shedding some tears, took her by the hand with an air that spoke him a gentleman. "Fair creature," said he, "I will assist and defend you, and that lovely friend that you support, with my life; fear not to descend with me into the vault, where I have lived above three tedious years, and where we may without fear of discovery talk our misfortunes over."

He took the loaf, and Catherina being now something recovered from her swoon, made way for him to go down before them with the light; at the bottom of the stairs they found a room all of stone, clean, though dismal, in which were three doors which opened into three other rooms like that; in one of these lay a great quantity of bones and skulls, which this poor hermit had cleared the other rooms of; in that he lived in, was a bed made of straw and rushes, into which he used to creep, covering himself with nothing else but an old mantle, in which he used to wrap himself in winter: near this his miserable bed, there lay two square stones, one about a foot higher than the other; the highest was his table to eat upon, the other his seat to sit upon; this with a poor lamp was all his furniture, except two earthen-dishes, and a stone-bottle that used to keep water for him to drink.

And now desiring his guests to sit down, lighting his lamp, he pulled a small bottle of arrack out of his pocket, desiring them to drink, which they did. Mean time viewing Catherina more attentively, he leaped up and caught her in his arms with such transport, that Angelina was amazed and terrified, fearing he had some ill design upon them; but she was quickly undeceived, for he cried out, "My Catherina! my angel! have I lived to embrace you again? Is it possible? and do I hold in my arms my wife? It is too much: Such joy is insupportable."

At these words, being extreme weak, he fainted, for he was even starved with this poor way of life, and grown a perfect skeleton. Catherina was so surprised, she could not utter one word; but Angelina poured some of the arrack into his mouth, and in some time he recovered, and the most passionate discourse passed between him and Catherina that can be imagined. For what joy could exceed hers to meet her dear husband again? She begged to know how he came to live in that place; and all that had passed since they were parted, which he related in these words, kissing her hands, and gazing upon her all the while, as if his glad soul, which seemed to sparkle in his eager eyes, would feast itself on that delightful object.

CHAPTER 16

My life, said he, the fatal day that we were parted, and you were sold to the cursed Bey of Tunis, who has no doubt enjoyed that lovely person (then he sighed deeply, and she wept) I was disposed of for a slave to an old Jew, who drove me home into the country before him, with my arms pinioned. Being come to his house, he put me into the garden to work, there I was made draw water, dig, and labor hard all day, at night chained like a dog in a hole under his summer-house on straw; my food and labor were so hard, that in a few days I fell sick of an ague and fever; so that fearing I should die, he took me into the house, making me wait at table, whet the knives, go on errands, and such trivial things; but my weakness increasing, I was at last confined to my bed.

This frightened him so, that he told me (finding I was a gentleman, and unfit for service) if I would write to my friends, and procure a tolerable ransom, he would let me go. Then I told him that there was a young gentlewoman who was taken with me in the same ship, and that if he could get me intelligence where she was, and find on what terms she might be freed, then I would send to Spain to my friends for a ransom for both, though they were but in mean circumstances; for I dared say no other, because the villain would have been extravagant in his demands: and I told him unless he could do this, I did not think it worth my while to write, or care what became of me. This vexed him horribly.

In short, I lay ill so long, that had not his daughter, a handsome Jewish maid, privately supplied me with some rich wines and good food, I had surely died: for though a kind of a doctor he employed, gave me some medicines that conquered my disease, yet I had never recovered strength enough to get away without her help; but being able to walk about, and little notice being taken of me by the servants, I left the house one evening, and resolved to get back near Tunis, where I hoped to get some news of you. This Jew's country-house was fifteen miles off it, and I was two days and nights a crawling to this ruinous place, into which I entered to rest myself, being quite spent. I had a bottle of wine, and some bread and meat tied up in a cloth in this little basket, in which I used to gather fruit for the table.

After I had eat and slept here, I began to consider what to do; if I entered the city, I should run the risk of being taken up perhaps and examined, and so be sent to prison for a runaway, or sent back to my master, which was almost as bad: so a thought came into my head, that if I could find means to subsist and live concealed in this place, I might have some fortunate opportunity of finding where you were. Then I began to view the place more narrowly, and found this door: I descended into the vault, but it was so dark I could not discern what was in it, but groping about, I thought I heard a groan, and turning my head, discerned the glimmering of a lamp in one of the inner rooms: I entered it, though in some disorder, and there I saw one of the most dismal objects that ever eyes beheld, it was an aged man dressed in this coarse coat that I have on, his beard reached to his waist, his bones appeared ready to start through his parched shriveled skin, his eyes were sunk, his voice failed, and he seemed to be in the last agonies of death, as indeed he was.

I could hardly recollect my spirits, I was so moved at this dreadful sight. He fixed his eyes upon me, and seemed desirous to speak to me. "In the name of Jesus," said I, "what are you that are thus come to dwell amongst the dead?" "That name," said he, "is sweet indeed; speak it again, dear Christian, and comfort my departing soul." At these words charity made me haste to give him some of my wine, of which he swallowed but a little with much difficulty; yet that a little revived him, and I begged him to get down some more. In fine, he was so refreshed, that I hoped I should have saved his life, but was deceived. "I know," said he, "your curiosity is great to know who I am, and the strange adventures that have brought me to this dismal place and end; and I will endeavor to reward your kindness, if I am able, with the story of my life."

"I was the eldest son of a noble family in Spain, it was my fortune to fall in love with a young lady, the daughter of a Grandee; I got her father's permission to court her, but was received but coldly; in fine, I found I had some rival who supplanted me in her affection, and made it my whole study to discover who he was; and it was not long ere I was satisfied that a young cavalier used to be admitted through the gardens frequently, in the dead-time of the night, to her apartment. I passionately loved her, and this discovery so enraged me, that I resolved to kill him. In short, I lay in ambush with three of my servants, in a grove behind the gardens, and saw him enter, leaving his horse and one servant to wait his coming out, which was not till the break of day. I advanced at the head of my servants, and shot him dead, and made off immediately without discovery, being masked; my coach waited about two miles off the place; so I quitted my horse, and went into it, reaching my own home in the city before it was broad day: by noon the news was spread all over the city that Don Emanuel de Cervantes my cousin-german was killed, but none could discover by whom. I concealed my thoughts, appearing much concerned for his death, and being unable to live at quiet without Belemante, I pressed for our marriage so earnestly, that her father consented, and we were joined by the sacred rites, not to be happy but wretched; for she was so sincere in her affection to her murdered lover, that she could never be happy with another; and having too well convinced myself the first night, that my bride was no virgin, I grew furiously jealous and unkind to her. This usage put her upon measures to be revenged: and her charms soon procured me such a rival, that I knew not how to cope withal; a Duke made me that modish thing a cuckold, and to prevent my having any opportunity of being revenged, not only came always well attended to my house, but procured me a great post in the army, which obliged me to be absent from home most part of the year; yet my wife lost no time, but cursed me with a child every year, so that I began to look on her as a vile strumpet, and the children as vipers and serpents produced by her lust and my dishonor.

At last I plotted the destruction of her and them, and having contrived this villany to destroy them, and ruin my own peace and soul, laid all things ready to escape from justice, I came home, and at one fatal supper in my wife's apartment, poisoned her and her three children. At midnight I took horse, and reached the next sea-port by day-break, where a bark lay which I had hired to carry me to England, having remitted a vast sum of money, thither in order to provide for me there, knowing I must never return to Spain again. I went on board, met with a great storm which drove us towards the Straits, where an Algerine pirate met with and took us; being brought to Tunis, I was sold for a slave to a Bassa, who kept me in extreme misery seven years: he being killed in the wars, I fell into the hands of his son, who was an officer of the guard to the King of Fez and Morocco; with him I traveled many thousand leagues, carrying burdens, and running by his horse's side. All this I looked upon as a just punishment inflicted upon me by divine justice for my enormous sins, and must confess the horrors of that guilt that loads my soul, were always more grievous to me than the bodily pains I suffered, though they were almost insupportable.

At last, quite wearied out and desperate, I fled over the mountains, and after wandering about in the disguise of a poor dervish, which is the habit I have on, by means of which I passed undiscovered to this place, in which I chose to reside, and have lived five whole years unmolested, I got my bread by begging in the adjacent city and suburbs, being held in great veneration by the common people, by reason of my dress, which made me pass for a religious Mahometan.

All this time I have been laboring to make my peace with God by prayers and tears, hoping to wash away my stains, and purify my conscience; this I hope through the merits of my savior. I have done: It is about ten days since, coming to my dismal cell, I saw two persons struggling as if one was going to rob or kill the other, and stepping in between them, one of them, which I suppose to be the thief, stabbed me into the thigh with a poisoned knife, as I since conclude, and then fled; the person I had rescued, seemed very thankful, and desirous to know who I was, to reward me; but I was shy of that, so he gave me a purse of gold and left me. I hastened home to dress my wound with some salve I had by me, but the next morning could not rise; I have lain here ever since in extreme torment, here had no food these three days past, and believe my thigh is mortified."

He related all this, often faltering in his speech, and groaning, nay fainting several times; but I spare to make particular mention of these things. He concluded thus: "And now," said he, "I shall die by a violent death, as those I murdered did; may God accept of these my sufferings and repentance here, in compensation of the ills I have done, and then I shall be happy." I kept him alive with the wine that night, but the mortification ended his unhappy life the next morning. I dragged his body into the next room, and shut up the door as close as I could, to avoid the stench of it, and concluded to live here, putting on his old coat as a sure disguise: I took the purse of gold also, which was a great help to me, and having dyed my face and hands with the juice of an herb to make me look thus tawny, have lived undiscovered all this time. I learned at my Jew-master's to make straw-hats, and baskets for to gather fruit in: these I make here in the heat of the day, and sell for bread and meat, which if I get none ready dressed, I broil upon some coals, making a fire of sticks in the mosque, in one corner of which I have made myself a kind of fire-place with stones; then I bring down some of the hot coals upon a tile into this place to warm and dry it, else I should die with the dampness of it.

I am so well acquainted with the country now, that I am confident I could find out some more commodious place to live in: but fearing to go farther off the city, and so be less likely to hear news of you, made me continue here; but since providence has been so merciful to bring you hither, you shall take up with this sad being some few days, till I can procure such a disguise for each of you as I have on, and color your faces like mine, which will wash off again; and then I'll provide some better place near the sea-side for us to dwell in, till God is pleased to send some ship to carry us off from this sad place.

The rich vests and turbans you have on would surely betray us; we will take the jewels off, and hide them in the vault among the dead bones, where none will seek them, and tomorrow I will buy two coats, and boots, with flannel to make you long tunics to your heels, to keep you warm, and hide your fine linen underneath; your heads shall be covered with flannel-hoods, like cowls, with straw-hats.

This resolved on, they sat down, and eat thankfully of the scraps he had brought home. Thus with a good conscience, men may live contented, nay be even happy in the most miserable circumstances. A charnel-house now entertains these two ladies, who are better pleased to eat scraps, and lie on straw and the cold stones, than dwell in a fine palace, and sleep on beds of down with infamy. After this poor repast, they prayed, and laid them down to rest, Don Sancho de Avilla having fastened the door of the vault within-side as he used to do, to prevent wild beasts from entering there.

The next morning he went to the city, and bought what they wanted, yet not at one place, but at several, for fear of suspicion, and returned soon; then they sat down to work, and made the flannel tunics and hoods, as he directed them; he had brought meat, and dressed it in the mosque above, whilst they worked in the vault below: by night they had finished their disguises; and he, impatient to remove them from that dismal place, went out after they had dined, and searching along the shore, found an old ruinous cottage on the side of a rock, so built in a cleft of the rock, that it was well screened from the bleak winds or parching sun, and so shadowed with trees that grew round about and over it, that it was not easily seen. No body lived in this place but an old fisherman and his wife. Don Sancho told them he was a poor dervish whose cottage was tumbled down, and if they would quit this for him and two more hermits to live in, he would pay them to their content; the poor devout peasants, reverencing his sacred person and profession, gladly consented: so he paid them a small matter, though to them a great sum, and they quitted the place, retiring to another cottage at a little distance from it; these poor people he employed to buy two quilts, some coverlets, and what else was wanting, to make this place a convenient cell for him and his two friends; and in three days time, all being ready, they removed in the dusk of the evening from their dismal vault to this clean wholesome cottage, where they lived for some months very happily, hiding the rich jewels and clothes in a hole in the rock. The poor fisher and his wife were very serviceable to them, fetching what they wanted, and supplying them with fish; and having a good strong boat, they hoped by his means to get to some ship, he having promised to go on board the first European ship he could get sight of at sea, for which service Don Sancho assured him, he would give them ten pieces of gold.

During the time of our female hermits' abode in this place, they never went into the town; but Don Sancho neglected not to go frequently to sell his straw baskets and hats, which the ladies learned to make with great dexterity; so that they made enough to supply them with bread and meat in way of exchange. And now he thought it would not be improper to convert some of the jewels into ready money, which might stand them in stead, in case they found cause to remove or means to get off. In order to this, he carried some of the jewels Catherina had brought away in the fine box she took out of the Bey's wardrobe, which they had broken open, and found to be full of jewels and gold; a few of these he went with to a Jew-merchant in the city, whom he told that he had found a box with these jewels, and some other things of value in it, on the sands, as he was walking on the sea-shore, and supposed to be part of some shipwreck: the Jew did not much trouble him with questions, but finding he should have them a good pennyworth, cared not how he came by them, and bid him a thousand pieces of gold, but Don Sancho insisted upon two thousand, to which the Jew at last agreed, and paid him down the money, the jewels being no doubt worth twice as much; but this sum was sufficient for our hermits. And now Don Sancho could boldly go to him, and buy what they wanted, without fearing to give occasion of suspicion, since the Jew would not wonder how he came by money.

All the diversion the hermits took, was to walk on the sea-shore in the evenings and early in the mornings, in hopes to discover some ship to get off. One morning, a dreadful storm having blown in the night, they went out to see what mischief was done; and Angelina being foremost, perceived something floating on the sea: she stood still to observe it, and soon saw it was a man, with his hands fast clenched on a chest, his habit was laced with silver; she cried out to Don Sancho to come to help this poor wretch: he ran, and stepping up to his middle in the water, caught hold of the chest and dragged it to shore. Then they took the man up, who appeared to be dead, but Don Sancho holding him up by the heels, the water poured out of his mouth in great quantity, after which some signs of life appeared; they carried him home to their cottage, gave him rack, and put him into a warm bed, and so brought him to life.

He was a very handsome gentleman, and his linen and clothes spoke him a man of no mean quality. Don Sancho left him with the ladies, whilst he called the fisherman to help bring the chest to the cottage, supposing it to contain something worth saving. The stranger viewed the ladies with wonder their strange habit and tawny complexions ill agreeing with the sweetness of their features, and delicate hands and limbs: he thought he knew one of them, yet was in doubt. Mean time they were very busy in tending him, giving him burnt wine, and talking in French to one another, a language he was no stranger to, for he was a French gentleman by birth. At last he addressed himself to Angelina in this manner; "Madam, if my eyes do not deceive me, I have the honor to know you, your name is Angelina, the unfortunate daughter of a mother who barbarously sent you out of France. Speak, are you a stranger to Monsieur du Pont?"

At this discourse she changed color, and shedding some tears, replied, "I am indeed the unfortunate Angelina, and too well know that name, since I am never like to see, or if I did, can never possess what I so dearly loved."

"Yes," said he, "you will I doubt not do both, for he is safely arrived in France, and a widower, having sought for you all over Canada and the West-Indies; he came home a little before I left France." Here he told her all the story of her mother's death, and the manner of their living together; that he was now possessed of a vast estate, and retired from the world on her account. By this time Don Sancho and the fisherman brought in the chest; and Angelina proceeded to ask the stranger who he was, not being still able to recollect.

He told her immediately that his name was Abrifeaux. "Good Heavens!" said she, "are you that charming gay young captain who used to visit and court my dear friend Madam de Belanger, when we were pensioners in the monastery together?"

"Yes," said he, "I am that unfortunate man, who have married and brought that lovely maid from France to lose her life I fear, and then it had been well for me to have perished with her; for if she's dead, life will be a hell to me. I beg you therefore to add to the charitable office you have done in saving me, by searching all the coast hereabouts carefully, for she was holding fast on the chest, when my senses forsook me, and then we were not far from the shore: I hope therefore that she may still be alive; if I do not find her, grief will perhaps finish that life that you have now restored me to. I saw a boat near us when I fainted, and conclude if she had been drowned, she would have kept her hold on the chest, as people generally do; for this reason I flatter myself the fisher-boat took her up, and neglected me, whom they might conclude dead, or that some wave might drive me out of their reach."

Don Sancho sent the old fisherman to make inquiry, who was acquainted with all the others on that coasl, the stranger being so weakhe could not rise. And now they intreated him to tell them his adventures and the manner of his coming to that coast; which he related in these words.

CHAPTER 17

After you, fair Angelina, left France, I continued my addresses to Madam Belanger, whose brother, soon after you were gone, went away for Virginia, being highly disgusted with his guardians, resolving to apply himself to an uncle he has there, who had considerable effects of his in his hands, and he persuaded himself would assist him against his other uncles: Madam de Santerell followed him, and no news of them has come to France since they left it. Madam Belanger was soon removed from St. Malos to Calais, and I following, she was sent to the Convent of Augustine Nuns at Paris.

Mean time my elder brother dying, I became master of a fortune sufficient to answer hers: so I applied myself not only to her obdurate uncles, but to the bishop and principal merchants, who importuned them to consent to our marriage, but to no purpose; for they were resolved never to part with her and her fortune, though I proceeded so far, that I offered to divide it with them; but this they rejected with a pretended scorn. In fine, I saw all I did was to no purpose, so I resolved to steal her away, and fly to Virginia to her brother, who being now come of age, might greatly assist me, as I will him.

I set out for Paris with this design, but was strangely disappointed when I came there, for she was removed thence to a house of her guardian's (an old stone building, strong as a little fort) in a village in Normandy. Here they placed her under a kind of guard, for they put an old hag in the chamber with her, who never let her stir out but on the leads (for it was the uppermost room in the house;) two stout surly fellows lived below, and took care of the gate. I took a private lodging in this village, disguised like a mean person, leaving my servants and horses at a market-town three miles off; and pretended to the old farmer where I lodged, that I had been sick, and was come to that place for my health, being a tradesman at Coutance; this passed very well with the country people. The house my dear Janetone was kept in, was moated round and had a draw-bridge, which was seldom let down but when any of the servants went out or in. I walked round it several days, to consider what course to take, and there I had the pleasure, or rather torment, of seeing my dear Janetone walking with the old hag upon the leads. I did not dare to make any sign to discover myself to her; and being convinced that it was impossible to get at her by fair means, I resolved to use force.

In order to which, I sent the old farmer's man to the market-town, with a letter to my valet-de-chambre, whom I had left with two footmen and four horses, to come to me next morning, which they accordingly did. I took them to a place in sight of the prison where my mistress was, and we stayed concealed under the shelter of some trees, till we saw one of the men-servants come out, the bridge being let down. We rode up with pistols in our hands, seized on the bridge, which my two servants kept, whilst my valet-de-chambre and I forced the servant at the gate to give us entrance; for I caught him by the throat, and clapping my pistol to his breast, bid him bring me to Madam Belanger, or I would kill him. He begged for mercy, and I held him by the arm, and ascended the stairs with him to the room where she was. You may believe she was extremely surprised at seeing a man enter the room thus rudely, but she quickly recovered her fright at the sight of me. The old hag screamed and roared like one distracted, but that I little regarded; so I bid my mistress follow me, and we ran down stairs. I mounted her upon my horse behind me, on which I had purposely put a pillion, and my men breaking down the draw-bridge, threw it into the moat, and so prevented our being pursued for some hours; in which time we made off to a curate's house cross the country, about twenty miles farther. Here we were married, and lay concealed for a month, in which time the search made after us was over, and they concluded we were gone out of the kingdom. Then having disguised her in man's clothes, and a ship and money, with bills of exchange, being got ready for us at Dieppe, we set out from the curate's, attended by two servants, and got safe off.

Now we thought ourselves happy, and had a prosperous voyage, till we came through the Straits; but then a dreadful storm arose, driving us on this coast; and our ship (which was but small) striking upon a rock, sprung a leak, and we had no way to save ourselves, but by getting into the long-boat: my dear wife was my chief care, I got her one of the first in, and the captain and several sailors and passengers leaped after in such disorder (all being willing to save their lives) that they over-set the boat, and we were all thrown into the merciless sea. I caught hold of my dear wife, and seeing a chest floating, and that we were not far from the shore, I caught hold of it, bidding her throw herself upon it: Thus we remained, till my strength was so spent, that I could no longer sustain the waves beating against me, and fainted at the moment I saw a fishing-boat making towards us; and now all my hope is, that she was taken into it.

Soon after he had ended his relation, the old fisherman entered, with the good news, that a fisherman standing on the shore, saw the lady taken up by the boat, from whence they threw a rope, which she caught hold of; and that the man on the chest was carried off towards the shore by the waves. He said the woman wrung her hands; and seemed to call after him; but that the boat made away out of his sight, from the shore. Monsieur Abrifeaux, lifting up his hands, cried, "My God, I thank thee with my soul, that her life is preserved: Let thy angels keep her safe, and direct me to her: strengthen my confidence in thee, that the improbability of our meeting again may not drive me to despair."

The hermits did all they could to comfort him, and procured a habit like theirs for him. They resolved to be gone the first opportunity, but he could not be persuaded to leave the place without his lady; nay, his impatience was such, that he often ventured out in a morning early, and would go many miles along the sea-shore, making inquiry of the fishermen: but alas! he was deceived in looking for her there, for she was otherwise disposed of. Some months passed in this manner, so that he began to despair of finding her, or they of getting thence; but Providence, whose ways are unsearchable, and always tend to our good, detained them there for the preservation of the virtuous Janetone.

Don Sancho one morning going out very early alone, to go to the city to sell his straw-ware, and buy provisions, as usual, passing by a wood, heard the voice of a woman making great lamentations in the French tongue: he turned aside to see if he could discover where she was, and following the voice, entered a great way into the wood, in the thickest part of which he perceived a woman sitting on the ground; she had a Turkish habit on, was very young and beautiful; she held her hands upon one of her legs, which was much swollen; her face was pale as death, her eyes sunk with weeping and famine; she looked upon him as a person resigned to death, and uttered not one word. He spoke to her in French, saying, "Madam, what ails you? how came you to this place? I am a Christian, and can help you."

"Alas!" said she, "I fear all help comes too late; I have been here three days with my leg broken, and have had neither food nor help, so am not able to move, or follow you: I fled from ruin and infamy, and have met death: I was saved from the merciless seas, to perish on the more inhospitable shore."

"Is not your name Abrifeaux?" said he. "Yes," said she. Here she swooned, he was troubled that he had nothing to give her, but was forced to run back to the fisherman's cottage, which was half a mile, yet nearer than his own; here he got some brandy, and made him follow him with a blanket. They ran all the way, and found her lying as dead, with her teeth clenched; he had much ado to get some of the brandy down her throat, but at last she began to breathe and move. Then they put her into the blanket, and carried her between them home to Don Sancho's, where the transported Abrifeaux was so divided between grief and joy, that he scarce knew what he said or did.

The ladies got her into bed, and gave her hot spoon-meat; but when they came to look upon her leg, they shrunk back amazed, for she had broken it short at the instep, the bone being split, came through; her leg and foot was so swelled, that had the best bone-setter in the world been there, he could not have set it at that instant. Catherina had some skill, she presently made a fomentation with herbs and wine, and applied poultices dipped therein to it, which gave the poor lady great relief in some hours: what to do more they knew not, for they did not dare to send for a Mahometan surgeon, and there was no Christians of that profession, and they all feared a mortification, but Monsieur Abrifeaux was almost distracted.

At last Don Sancho went to the Jew, and told him he had occasion for a surgeon, and desired his assistance. He told him, a friend of his had bought a Christian slave of that profession, who had been surgeon to a French ship; he would direct and recommend him to that friend. He went with a letter from this Jew to the other, who freely lent him his slave. So they went together, and Don Sancho talking with him by the way, found he was surgeon to the ship which brought Angelina from Canada. He acquainted him with her being in his house, and his own story, not fearing to be discovered by a Christian, whom he offered to redeem from slavery of the Jew; an offer the other gladly accepted of, no question; for though we often live as ill as heathens, who profess ourselves Christians, and whilst we live together are often at variance; yet none but such as have experienced it, can tell the joy and comfort poor Christians find, in meeting and conversing together when in slavery, and amongst Turks and heathens; then true charity glows in their breasts, and they gladly assist one another to the utmost of their power.

This surgeon was caressed by all, but especially by Angelina, who knew him to be a very honest gentleman. He dressed the poor lady, and miraculously restored her leg to such a state, that in six weeks she could walk with a crutch, though never able to go upright, but was ever lame, it being impossible to cure it otherwise, having lain so long without help. Angelina asked him what was become of the captain? He told her he was dead, he believed, of the wounds he received in the fight; a just reward for his crimes in using her as he had done. And now Madam Abrifeaux being able, acquainted them how she came into this condition, and the occasion of her flying to the wood where Don Sancho found her.

CHAPTER 18

Being pulled into the boat (said she) by means of the rope they threw out to me, I expected them (having shown so much charity to me) to have made after you (addressing herself to her husband;) but they seemed deaf to my entreaties; neither did they understand me, I believe, because they were strangers to my language. They made away for Tunis, to which they were going, it being a fishing-boat belonging to a Bashaw who lives there, and sent them out the day before to get fish for his table, as his custom was. They certainly imagined they had got a prize in me, seeing me young and tolerably handsome. When they had brought me to shore, they led me directly to the Bashaw's (their master's) house, where I was delivered to a black, who seemed mighty glad, and viewed me so curiously, that my face was overspread with blushes. By him I was led to a fine apartment, where an old maid-servant, who spoke French, came to me; the grief and surprise I was under made me glad to meet with somebody, to inform me what I was to be done with: I asked her many questions, and was answered, that I was to be mistress to one of the handsomest and most powerful men in the place, that he was his prince's chief favorite; in short, she praised him up to the skies. I told her I was already married, and must rather die, than admit of another's embraces. She laughed at that, and taking off my wet clothes, brought me up a Turkish dress.

Thus I remained many days confined in this place, being furnished with all necessaries of food, habit, and lodging; in which time walking in the gardens, I saw and conversed with some of those unfortunate women who had been purchased for his pleasures, Europeans, now made slaves to the insolent Mahometan, who was at this time at a country-house about two miles distant from the wood in which Don Sancho found me, so that it was some months before I was exposed to the lascivious view. During my abode in this place I made some attempts to escape, but could never effect it, for the slaves so narrowly watched us, that there was no hopes of getting away. And now being almost overwhelmed with sorrow, I applied myself to God to deliver me. Indeed, I wondered that I continued so long without seeing this tyrannical Algerine; but at last I learned the reason, he was sick of a tertian ague and fever all that time: at last being recovered, he ordered me to be brought to him, to his country-house, having had such an advantageous character given him of me, that he was impatient to see me.

I had contracted a kind of friendship with a young creature, who had been brought there at ten years old; her name was Henrietta Belhush, a French peasant's daughter; who being god-daughter to a lady, whose husband was a rich merchant, and went to settle in the West-Indies with his family, she took this beautiful girl along with her, and the ship being unfortunately taken, and brought into Tunis, she was sold to this Bashaw, whose mistress she had been five years when I came to that unhappy place. She was fair as an angel, witty, and highly sensible of her misfortune. She had brought him a daughter, which was carried away from her soon after it was born. She pitied me extremely, and assured me that it was almost impossible to escape thence. She seemed resigned to her misfortunes, and said, since God had been pleased to suffer her to be reduced to such a way of life, where she could have no opportunity of practicing her religion, or avoiding the infidel's embraces, she hoped he would not lay any thing to her charge as a crime, since it was compulsion, not choice. But all her arguments seemed weak to me, and I resolved on death, rather than to yield.

At last, one morning the old French woman entered my chamber, and bid me prepare myself to go to the great man, whose favorite I was to be. She brought me a rich habit and linen, and dressed me to all the advantage such a pagan habit could be put on with, whilst I stood weeping, careless of what she did, and meditating what to do. At last she threw a veil over me, and led me through the garden to a kind of horse-litter, into which the black slave put me. I perceived that there were seven or eight ill-looked slaves to guard me, so that it was in vain to resist. I was about three hours upon the road, and had refused to eat any thing before I set out; so that I was so faint when they came to take me out, that two of them were obliged to lead me into the house, which was a kind of earthly paradise, adorned with fine paintings, and such furniture, that I was surprised. Being conducted to a delicate chamber, where there was a bed made after the European fashion, and velvet stools and chairs, things very uncommon in these parts of the world; they left me, and in a few moments after a gentleman, in a rich night-gown and turban, entered: he was tall, slender, and delicately shaped, his eyes were black and shining, his skin moderately fair, his air and mien so soft and engaging, that I stood confounded.

At these words Monsieur Abrifeaux reddened; she perceiving it, with a smile said, "My dear, don't be jealous, for his beauty and persuasions did him no further service with me, but to raise my pity; for I soon perceived he was a European, and had bought his greatness here by renouncing his faith." He bowed, and stood looking upon me for some time without speaking; then, like a man wakened from a pleasant dream to substantial joy, he caught me in his arms, and said in French, "Fame has done you wrong, sweet creature; you are fairer than fancy could conceive; take to your arms a man that adores you, and knows how to value such a treasure; no barbarian or fierce moor, but one who was born in the politest part of the world: I am an Italian, whom injuries drove hither; who being ruined by my fellow-Christians, have fled for succor to barbarians, who have advanced and made me great enough to make you as happy as the world can make you."

My soul was filled with horror at these words. "Have you renounced your savior," said I, "and think a Christian can look upon you without abhorrence? My religion and honor are so dear to me, that I will die for either; and though I am in your power (as you imagine) whilst I remain firm in this resolution I am safe, and your attempts are vain." He used all the persuasions possible to gain me, nay, stooped to beg and pray; but finding me still inflexible, and growing faint, being still weak with his late illness, he called for wine, sherbet, and sweetmeats, courting me to eat and drink; but I refused. Then he asked me if I designed to be my own murderer, and damn myself? I answered, "No; but that I did not think it safe to eat and drink with a person who had base designs upon my virtue, and might, perhaps, deprive me of my reason by some stupifying drug, and ruin me: therefore I would abstain from eating till providence supplied me with some wholesome bread and water, or any thing that might satisfy hunger without danger."

He seemed surprised at my being so resolute, and no doubt but his conscience pricked him when he saw me so well perform my duty, which he had through cowardice and ambition acted contrary to. At last he took leave, bidding me reflect, that no human power could free me from him; that I must at last yield to his desires; that he would much rather gain me by courtship, than force; but if I continued obstinate, he must be obliged to constrain me to be kind: then he left me, a slave keeping the door. This civility, I believe, was owing to his weakness; but being now left alone, I sat down in a chair, and fell into a serious consideration of my wretched condition: I had no weapon to defend myself, or harm him; the doors were guarded; then I viewed the windows, and they were so high, that a leap from thence seemed to threaten certain death: I disputed in my conscience the lawfulness of such an action.

Thus I sat till evening, being often interrupted by his officious slaves, who brought me choice wines and presents from him, all which I refused; yet at last fearing want of sustenance would render me unable to resist him if he offered force, or faintness seize my spirits, and deprive me of my reason, I made the slave that brought in the wine, drink a glass of it before me, and then I took two glasses full myself, and eat some bread. When it grew dark they urged me to go to bed, but I refused. They brought in two wax lights, and retired, shutting the door; and now I trembled, fearing what followed. About midnight the apostate Bashaw entered the chamber, and fastening the door, came to me, using all the softest persuasions and entreaties; in short, finding me deaf to all his solicitations, he proceeded to use force; but then some kind angel sure assisted me, for I grew strong, and he soon tired, renewed his entreaties. At last he swooned at my feet, and then being distracted with my fears, I resolved to use those happy moments; so without standing to deliberate, I caught the sash off that tied his night-gown, and fastening one end to one of the bars of the windows, slid down; but that being not above three yards long, I fell down from a great height, and lay for some time quite stunned; but recovering, found I had not broken my bones, and rising on my feet, fled towards the next wood, it being a very moon-light night. I thought it not so far off as it proved, for it was near two miles, as I guess, and I had hardly strength left to reach it, but fear drove me on. When I entered the wood I was filled with more dreadful apprehensions, and fancied the wild beasts would devour me; to avoid which I got up into a tree, whose trunk, being old and hollow, I easily climbed. There I seated myself, and passed the remainder of the night till daybreak; but then I feared to descend, lest I should be pursued; nor did I know where to go. Whilst I was thus musing sleep prevailed over thought, and I fell into a slumber, and dropped down from the tree, which fall broke my leg. What I endured for three days that I lay there, you may imagine: I expected nothing but death, as I had reason to do; but providence preserved and relieved me by your means, for which I will be thankful whilst I live.

All the company joined in praises to God, and were filled with admiration. They passed the time for some weeks very agreeably, till the good old fisherman, whom they had converted to the Christian faith, together with his wife, acquainted them, that he had that morning met at sea with a Spanish ship, had been aboard it, and informed the captain of their being there: that he had promised to send his long-boat that night to a creek behind the rocks, to fetch them. "It is," said he, "a ship of good force, and fears no pirate, being well armed and manned." Don Sancho, on this news, went away to Tunis, and gave his friend the surgeon notice, who went back with him. The ladies in the mean time packed up their jewels, money, and some linen; and all being ready, they went away to the creek in the dusk, and waited the boat's coming. They offered to take the fisherman and his wife along with them, but they chose to end their lives in their own country, pleading their age: so they left them all their furniture, and twenty pieces of gold, a sufficient provision for them. The ship's boat came about eleven of the clock at night, and carried them off safely to the ship, Don Sancho promising to assist Angelina and the surgeon to return to France by land, and he and Catherina doubted not of a good reception from his friends at Madrid. Besides, the two ladies had brought such a treasure in jewels from the Bey's seraglio, that (being divided) was sufficient to provide for them all. Monsieur Abrifeaux and his lady were presented with a part of them, and his chest having been saved, was a provision for them; and they were prevailed upon to desist from their intended voyage to Virginia, Angelina promising, that Monsieur du Pont should stand by them against her unjust guardians; so they determined to go home to France with her. The Spanish captain received them with transport, and now they had leisure to entertain him with an account of all their strange adventures.

They arrived at Barcelona in good health, paid part of their jewels there, highly rewarded the captain, and Don Sancho's friends provided nobly for him and Catherina, who wrote to her parents at Venice an account of all her sufferings, and safe return to Europe. The French ladies and gentlemen stayed some days to recover themselves of the fatigue of their voyage, and then set out for France, promising never to forget the civilities they had received, and the friendship they had all contracted with one another in their misery. And now it is fit that we leave the barbarous Algerines, and return to Charlotta, and the unhappy Belanger, whom we left traveling to Virginia through Carolina.

CHAPTER 19

Monsieur Belanger and his generous kinsman Montandre, with the hermit Monsieur du Riviere, came safe to Virginia, where they were gladly received by the old gentleman and his new wife. Belanger was much pleased that she was now his aunt, and Montandre liked her well enough for a mother-in-law; yet she could not look upon her nephew without blushes and some kind of disorder. This was observed by her husband, and he began to wish his kinsman thence. He well knew that she married him in a pique, not out of affection.

In short, having been informed of all that had befallen him and his son in their voyage to the Island of St. Domingo, he calmly advised him to return to France, having honorably accounted with him for all the moneys and effects left in his hands, and made him a handsome present of sugars, tobacco, and other commodities which that country produces, to a great value; saying, "Nephew, I always designed you something, and though I have now a prospect of more children, yet I will do what I intended; you are now of age, and your guardians can no longer detain you from your own; it is time you should settle in the world, and the young woman you liked being disposed of to another, you must use your reason; conquer that passion which is now unlawful and injurious to your repose, and look out for a wife in your own nation, to bring posterity to keep up your name, and be comforts to you in your declining years." Belanger thanked him for his good advice and present, but was determined not to follow his counsel, though Monsieur du Riviere pressed him extremely to go with him to France; but Belanger would not consent to leave Charlotta behind.

Young Montandre did likewise spur him on to let him go back to the island to inquire after her: but alas, he had another design than that only in view; he had seen the charming Teresa, Don Medenta's sister, and her bright image so filled his soul, that he could not rest. We easily consent to what we desire. Belanger deals with the captain that carried them thither before, to go back again with Montandre. Meantime, he finding his uncle look cold upon him, invited Monsieur du Riviere, no ship being at that time ready to go for France, to go with him to see another plantation of his uncle's, and view the country.

The ship goes off with Montandre, much against his father's will; but he arrived safe at the island, and resolved to lie on board the ship every night, and not take a lodging on shore, for fear of discovery; in the day he ventured to walk about the town, and went to the great church to mass on the next Sunday after his arrival. There he saw the charming Charlotta, with her little son and daughter standing by the governor her father-in-law, dressed in a widow's dress, and Teresa in deep mourning. This was a very agreeable sight no doubt to him; he did not dare to venture to speak to her, but was fain to wait for an opportunity some other time, which he supposed would not be extremely difficult, now Don Medenta was gone; but he was mistaken, for he had engaged his father on his death-bed to prevent, if possible, her ever seeing Belanger again.

"My dear lord and father," said he, "he is the cause of my death, he ruined my repose, and if he returns, will rob my dear children of their mother; her affections are still inclined to him. I have brought her to the Catholic faith, he is a Huguenot, and will seduce her from her religion and children; do not let my fortune serve to enrich my hated rival, nor my children be wronged." He likewise charged Charlotta, as she valued his soul's repose, not to marry him, or leave that island and his children.

Thus the revengeful Spaniard, even in death, continued to hate his brave rival, who had a prior right to her heart, and endeavored to prevent his happiness, even when he could no longer enjoy her himself. For these reasons the governor, who was inconsolable for the loss of his son, desired Charlotta to live in the castle with him, where she was respected as a queen, and had all the reason in the world to be contented.

Teresa, who was courted by the greatest persons in the island, kept her company, and there was the greatest friendship imaginable between them. Teresa had not as yet felt Cupid's tyranny; she seemed invincible to love.

Montandre having waited some days in vain for an opportunity to speak to Charlotta, grew weary, and resolved to give her a letter in public. He thought in himself, she is now a widow, and free to choose whom she pleases: why should I fear to remind her of her vows and engagements with my friend? He dressed himself very fine the next festival day, and went to mass earlier than before, and there waited till they all came; then he went boldly up to Charlotta, and with a profound bow, presented the letter to her: this he did with such a grace and mien, that Teresa, looking upon him, was seized with such an unusual liking to him, and so disordered, that she could scarce conceal it; and love at this fatal moment entered her breast.

He withdrew to the other side of the altar so soon as he had delivered the letter, and there placed himself on his knees right against them, with design to observe Charlotta's countenance, by which he hoped to judge of her sentiments in relation to his friend, as likewise to have the pleasure of looking often upon the charming Teresa, to whom his eager glances spoke his passion, whilst her unguarded looks and blushes assured him he was taken notice of. Meanwhile the governor observed him, and watched Charlotta; who having looked on the superscription of the letter, guessed that it brought news of Belanger, and remembered Montandre's face.

This threw her into a mighty disorder; she put the letter into her pocket, not daring to peruse it in so public a place; but the distraction of her mind caused her in a few minutes to faint. This confirmed the governor in his suspicions, and he whispered one of his gentlemen, whom he beckoned to him, to take care that gentleman was secured as he went out of the church, and kept under a guard till he examined him.

Prayers being ended, he gave Charlotta his hand to lead her to the coach, so that she had no opportunity to speak to Montandre. A young cavalier, who courted Teresa, did the same by her, inflamed with jealousy at her behavior towards the stranger, who imprudently followed them, in hopes to speak to one of the ladies; but he was seized at the church-door as they were going into the coach; he struggled, and demanded a reason of the soldiers and gentlemen that laid hands upon him, but could get no other answer but that it was the governor's order: so he was carried to a room in the castle, and kept till the governor, having conducted the ladies to their chamber, came and examined him, asking him what the letter contained that he had given his daughter-in-law, whence he came, and who sent him: to all which he answered boldly, and told the truth, saying, "My lord, I do not think I have done anything but my duty. She is a widow, was promised to my kinsman before, and forced unjustly from him; he is her equal, and her first choice, and I cannot imagine why you should detain her from him."

"Your friend," replied the governor fiercely, "by his imprudent coming hither, ruined my son's peace, and broke his heart; he begged me with his dying breath never to let him see her more, to rob his children of her presence, whom I will never let her carry hence; and he has bound her by the strictest injunctions never to marry again; and to be brief with you, I am determined, if ever he sets foot on this island again, to take such measures to secure him, that it shall never be in his power to disturb her or me any more. As for you, I'll try whether a prison cannot hold you, and if you escape hence again it shall be my fault." At these words he left the room, and Montandre was hurried away that night under a guard to a strong prison into which they used to put criminals of state, ten miles from the town; here he was lodged in all appearance for his life.

Charlotta, so soon as her father-in-law left her with Teresa, opened the letter and read it aloud to her; she could not conceal her joy to hear Belanger was alive and constant. "Ah! my dear sister," said she, throwing her arms about her neck, "why did your revengeful brother lay me under such cruel obligations not to marry this dear man, to whom my faith and heart was given before? He forced me from him. Is it just, that having been a faithful wife to him, I should not be at liberty to dispose of myself to him to whom I do of right belong now he is dead?"

Your generous soul, though yet a stranger to love, is sensible of pity, and cannot but compassionate my distress, my soul being divided betwixt duty to my dead lord, and affection to my living." Teresa embracing her with tears, replied, "Alas, my sister, I participate of your griefs, and fear that I am born to be unhappy too, I love the generous Montandre; his person, and noble friendship to Belanger charms me; and if I am not deceived, I am not indifferent to him. I will do all that I am able to assist you, but I fear my father will undo us both; I saw his furious looks, and fear the effect of his resentments: just as we entered the coach, I saw the people gather in a crowd, and fear some mischief."

As they were talking, Teresa's woman, Emilia, entered as pale as death: "Madam," said she, "there is a strange gentleman seized, and brought under a guard into the castle, I saw him carried along just now up the great square." This news extremely alarmed them, and confirmed their fears; they employed Emilia, not daring to be too inquisitive themselves, to get intelligence, for she was mistress to Don Fernando the governor's gentleman, who had the charge of Montandre; but he, setting out with him that night for the prison to see him secured there, she could get no account till the next morning, when she got the secret out of Fernando where he was.

This news overwhelmed the ladies with grief, and Charlotta grew so incensed, that she quarrelled with her father-in-law, complaining that she was not treated as she ought to be, and that if the gentleman was not freed, she would complain to the King of Spain, that she had been taken away from Belanger by fraud, and compelled to marry Don Medenta; that she was a subject of England, and though his daughter-in-law, yet that he had no power to command or restrain her from going off the island, and marrying whom she pleased.

This so enraged the governor, that he told her, that since he found she had so little sense of her honour, and respect for her husband's memory and her children's good, or his dying commands, he would take care to keep her to her duty, and prevent her disgrace; that Belanger was of too mean a rank to be received in the place of that noble Spaniard his dear son, who was descended from an illustrious family, and had demeaned himself in marrying her; that he had hitherto treated her for his sake with too much indulgence, which he perceived she had no grateful sense of; that Montandre, though a good friend to Belanger, yet was a venturous fool to return thither on so vile an errand, as to bring love-letters to another man's wife; that he began to doubt whether his son had died fairly, or not, and to suspect she had by some cursed slow poison destroyed him, else they could not have known the time when it was fit to come to her, and knew she was a widow: in short, he loaded her with bitter reproaches and taunts, and confined her to her apartment under a guard, suffering none to go near her but Teresa and some few of his relations, who teased her continually with the respect she owed her dead husband, and how she ought never to marry another inferior to him.

The governor little suspected his daughter was any ways concerned in Montandre's welfare; but, alas, she was as much afflicted as Charlotta, and ventured to send Emilia with a purse of gold to him. He would have sent a letter back, but was denied pen, ink and paper. Emilia lent him her table-book, in which he wrote a most passionate letter to Teresa, declaring his love, and begging her to let the captain who brought him thither, be informed of what had happened to him, and sent back to Belanger to warn him not to come thither. On the receipt of this letter, Teresa dispatched Emilia to the captain, who presently weighed anchor, and set sail for Virginia, to carry these joyful and sad tidings to Belanger; first that Charlotta was a widow, and next that Montandre was in prison, and she under a guard on his account.

Belanger in a short time was informed of all, the ship coming safe to Virginia; and no persuasion of his uncle, aunt and friends could deter him from going over to the island, to demand his lady, and release his friend: but the captain of the ship refused to go back, saying he was sure he should be imprisoned and lose his ship. And now it was some months before he could get a vessel to carry him; during which the governor was informed by his spies of Emilia's visits to Montandre in the prison, and caused him to be secretly removed to the old castle where he had been before a prisoner; there the commanding officer had such a strict charge given him to take care of him, that he was secured from any possibility of an escape, not being ever permitted to go on the battlements, but confined to a chamber with two centinels at the door night and day, being relieved every four hours.

The haughty governor having thus secured him, laid wait to catch Belanger, not doubting but he would soon follow his friend, when he heard the news from the Virginia captain, of whose departure out of the port he had had intelligence, and would have stopped the ship, which he had a good pretence for, it being a time of war between the English, French and Spaniards; but only he concluded it best to let it go to fetch Belanger.

Charlotta fell sick, and Teresa grew very melancholy and much altered; no news could be got of Montandre. At length she fell dangerously ill, insomuch that her life was in danger, and being light-headed, called perpetually on Montandre. This opened the governor's eyes, who finding she loved this stranger, lost all patience. She was now his only child, and all his ambitious hopes were comprehended in her being nobly disposed of. The noblest and wealthiest gentlemen in the place made their addresses to her, and would have been proud of having her: but she was attached to a man whose father was only a merchant, married to a second wife, by whom he had younger children to lessen his fortune; besides he was a Protestant, and that alone was enough to make him reject the match; in fine, he was at his wits end; the physicians told him medicines could do no good, he must resign her to death, or bring the person to her whom she loved.

This expedient was death to him, yet he could not consent to lose his darling, the lovely Teresa; at last he sent for Montandre, who was brought pinioned under a guard like a criminal, and expected nothing but death; he had been sick a considerable time of an ague and fever, which was turned to a yellow jaundice, so that he was so altered, that his friends would scarce have known him.

Being brought to the castle, and carried up into a room, the governor came to him with looks that expressed the inward distraction of his mind.

"Stranger," said he, "what would you do to gain your freedom?"

"Nothing," he replied fiercely, "that should be injurious to my honour or conscience. I am now indifferent to life, and would not thank that man who, having injured me, should ask me pardon and release me; you may use me as you please, you have treated me so ill already, that I expect neither justice nor favour from you."

The governor could not but admire Montandre's bravery in secret, but yet seemed angry; and answered, "Sir, do you consider whom you speak to, and that your life's at my disposal?"

"Yes I do, sir," said Montandre, "and have spoke my thoughts."

"Well sir," said the governor, "I acknowledge I have used you somewhat roughly; but had you lost such a son as I have, killed by your friend's rash attempt, which has broke my son's heart and Charlotta's peace, you would doubtless have acted like me; but I have now but one daughter" (here he wiped off the falling tears) "do you respect her?"

Montandre alarmed at these words, answered hastily, "Yes, and honour her above the world, nay dare to tell you that I love her, and that it is my greatest ambition to die at her feet, if fate would permit me; nor is there a thing on earth for which I would wish to live beside her self."

"For her sake," answered the governor, "you shall not only live, but be freed." At these words he took him by the hand, and calling in a servant, who unbound him, he led him to Teresa's chamber, who was so weak that she had been many days confined to her bed.

"Here my dear child," said the governor, "is the gentleman you so much respect; I shall leave you together." He was so disordered, being forced to stifle his resentments and constrain his pride, that he immediately withdrew.

Teresa lifting up her eyes, viewed Montandre with much concern, unable to speak, his altered face too well informed her of the treatment he had met withal; whilst he seeing her, whom he so dearly prized, in a condition so unlikely to recover, fetched a deep sigh, and falling on his knees by the bed, caught her hand, and pressing it to his lips, said with a low voice, "Must we then meet to part so soon again, and must death deprive us of that happiness we might now possess? Speak, divine creature, what hopes?"

"If," said she, "there be a cordial to restore me to health again, it is the sight of you, a blessing I despaired of. Say, does my cruel father relent, will he consent to make us happy? and has he granted you your liberty? If so, I will endeavour to live."

At these words, he fell into a great transport; and the governor entering, said a great many obliging things to him. In fine, Teresa in a short time recovered, and was married to Montandre, on his promising to reside there, and not return to Virginia to live.

But poor Charlotta, though glad of her sister's good fortune, and pleased to converse with Montandre, of whom she learned all that had befallen the unfortunate Belanger, yet could get no satisfaction, or find means to go to him, the governor having took such measures that no person could enter or go out of the sea-ports without his knowledge. Montandre could not as yet propose going to Virginia, but supposed his friend would shortly arrive, and that Teresa's interest, and his, with his father-in-law, was sufficient to procure his consent to Belanger's marriage with Charlotta. Thus they flattered themselves: but a Spaniard's revenge must be gratified; and they never, or very rarely forgive an injury.

Belanger having procured a vessel to carry him, and taking a considerable sum of money from his uncle, set sail from Virginia, and arrived at the island of St. Domingo about a month after Montandre's marriage. He no sooner set his foot upon the shore, filled with expectations of seeing his dear Charlotta, but he was seized by ruffians, bound hand and foot, and carried aboard another ship, where he was put in irons, and sailed the next morning, but he knew not whither. The same night that he was seized, the captain of the ship that brought him, received a message from the governor to depart the island that moment, or expect to be treated as an enemy, and his ship to be seized. He obeyed immediately, finding that neither threats nor entreaties could avail him. This news never reached Charlotta's ear; and poor Belanger, overwhelmed with despair, was carried up the great River Oroonoko, and set on shore amongst the savages, being carried in a boat up to the River Paria, where he expected nothing but to be murdered, and eaten by the barbarous Indians, who dwelt in huts, and are under no civil government. They speak no language, but a jargon that no European understands.

The cruel Spaniards unbound him, gave him a sword, a gun, and a horn of powder, with a pouch full of bullets and shot; telling him if he offered to make the least attempt to follow them, they would kill him on the spot. He little regarded what they said, being both weak and overwhelmed with the dreadful prospect he had before him of being left in a strange place, from whence there was no probability of escaping; a place which we Europeans are little acquainted with amongst savages, whose language and customs he was an entire stranger to, that he sat down upon the ground, and casting his eyes round wept bitterly: then looking up to heaven, besought God to look upon him, and deliver him from the miseries of life.

Whilst he was thus employed, the villains retreating to their boat were set upon by a party of savages, about a hundred in number, many of whom fell by the Spaniard's shot, who discharged their guns and pistols at them, which obliged the Indians to give back. The Spaniards being but eight in number, and some of them wounded, retired towards the shore to get into their boat; but, to their great surprise, found it gone; for their companions that were left to take care of it, being shot at with arrows by the savages, who from the rocks shot down upon them, concluded their companions dead, and made off to their ship with all the speed they were able.

The cruel Spaniards now too late repented the wicked deed they had done, and seeing death at hand, trembled at future punishments; despair urged them on, and they turned back and pursued their enemies, who led before them to the place where poor Belanger, roused with the noise of their guns and swords, was standing as a man who was prepared for death, and unconcerned at whatever happened: but when they called to him to help them, crying forgive, and join with us; Christianity, and the generosity of his great soul, made him forget the injuries they had done him; and like a lion roused from his den, fell on the savages till they had all left the place. Then thinking it unsafe to pursue them further, he advised the Spaniards to retreat towards the river under the covert of some rock; they consented, and acted thither, there they found a great cavern in the side of a rock, into which they entered with joy, and being quite spent; and three of them dangerously wounded, they sat down on the ground to rest, destitute of food or any necessaries.

That night the three wounded men expired; a sad admonition to the rest, who were conscious they deserved no less. They were now sincerely penitent, and consulted with Belanger, whom they resolved to obey in all things, what was best to be done; they knew they could not live without provisions, and though they hoped the boat would return to fetch them, yet that being uncertain, they must find some way to subsist.

At last they resolved to go out of this dismal place before it was broad day, and if possible seize upon one of the huts of the savages, and secure them, and so keep them as hostages, sending one at a time to fetch food for them, and by signs threaten to kill the rest if he failed to return. They charged their fire-arms, and crept along the shore till they came to a hut, into which they entered, and found two savages, a woman, three children, and an European man, as his complexion showed, asleep; they seized the savages, but for the white man, who appeared to be of a great age, he arose and embraced them, crossing himself; and lifting up his hands as a man over-joyed, he spoke to them in the Latin tongue, desiring to know who they were and whence they came.

The Spaniards, afraid to speak the true cause of their coming thither, said they were come on shore in their boat in search of fresh water, and being set upon by the savages, had been detained there whilst the boat went off; those they left in it being as they suppose frightened away by the noise of their guns. Then the old man spoke to the Indians in their tongue, and they immediately fell at the Spaniards feet, kissing them, and bowing down their heads in token of obedience. The old man told Belanger that he had lived twenty years in that country; that he was a Benedictine monk, born at Valladolid in Spain, and thence sent to Peru, from whence he had traveled to this place by land; that he had learned the language of these savages, and living amongst them, gained their esteem, and converted many to Christianity; that these poor savages were some of them, with whom he chose to live, being very honest people; that he would undertake they should supply all their wants, and be very serviceable to them; that the savages they had fought with were the enemies of the prince that governed that part of the country, and used frequently to invade him, and carry off some of his people, whom they eat, as his subjects did them; but that now he had persuaded a great many from doing it, and pretty well broke them of those barbarous customs. Then he desired the Spaniards to sit down with him, and take some refreshment without fear. After which he said he would conduct them to a place where they might live securely, till he could find means to procure their return to the Island of St. Domingo or Virginia, offering to be their guide to Cartagena, from whence they might get shipping to either place.

Belanger returned him a thousand acknowledgments, and in his soul greatly admired the providence of God, but wanted an opportunity to inform him of the Spaniards' villainy in bringing him thither, and to warn him not to be too free in discovering any secret retreat to them, which he was desirous to conceal, though his countrymen; for though they appeared sincerely penitent, yet he feared to trust himself with them to return to the Island of St. Domingo, resolving to go to

Virginia, and not venture to go there any more; concluding in himself, that if Charlotta's affection for him continued sincere, she would now, being a widow, find means to get away and come to him thither; and that if at his return to Virginia, he could hear nothing of her nor his dear friend Montandre, he would apply to the Spanish Viceroy at Mexico for justice; and being a native of France, he doubted not of obtaining it, since France and Spain were at peace.

He and the rest sat down with the good monk; the poor savages, who were by profession fishermen, set bread and cold dressed fish before them, with some meat and broth, which they had boiled the day before for the humble priest and themselves; this they had warmed over a fire which they made in the hut with a few stones set in form of a hearth, with a hole made in the ground, setting the pot on the stones, and making a fire underneath: they gave them also drink and rum, which greatly refreshed them. Belanger whispered the monk that he wanted to speak with him alone; he took the hint, and after eating, advised the Spaniards to lie down on the clean straw which the poor savages had laid for them in one corner of the hut, the only bed he and they had used to lie upon; "there," said he, "you may repose yourselves, whilst your leader and I discourse." They readily complied, glad to take some rest.

So he and Belanger walked out over a hill, then they descended into a fine valley, at the bottom of which was a little kind of copse or thicket, composed of stately tall trees and close quickset hedges. By the way Belanger told him his story; and the monk detesting their baseness, told him he should return no more to them, but abide with those that he had placed in that little cell to which he was going to carry him: "there you will find," said he, "a gentleman and lady whose conversation will make you think the time no way tedious whilst you stay here; it is a month since they were cast away upon this shore, and by my means, through the mercy of God, preserved as you have been.

I heard a dreadful storm in the dead of the night, and walking out on the shore so soon as day-break to see what mischief that sad night had done, discerned at some distance two women, one richly dressed, the other like her servant, wringing their hands, and lamenting over a person who lay on the sands, as I supposed, dead; the lady expressed the most extravagant concern that ever I beheld. I made what haste I could to their assistance, and at my approaching her was extremely surprised; she was young, and fair as an angel, her hair was hanging loose, and wet as was her habit, but she had a necklace and pendants of diamonds, with a stomacher that dazzled my eyes; she was dressed in a Spanish dress, her vest was black velvet, her petticoat gold tissue, bracelets of pearl; and in fine, I never saw a person of greater beauty, or who appeared more like a woman of quality than the distressed Elvira, for that is her name: the man that lay at her feet as dead, appeared her equal in all kinds; he was young, handsome, richly dressed, and seemed just drowned.

I stayed not to deliberate, but lifted him up, saying in Spanish, which I supposed she spoke, 'God comfort and help you, sweet lady, has this gentleman been here in this condition any time?' 'Oh no,' said she, 'he is just cast upon the shore.' Then said I, there is hopes; I immediately turned his head downwards, and a great deal of water pouring out of his mouth, he showed some signs of life. Having thus given his stomach some relief by this discharge of the water, I set him upright on the ground, chafed his temples, and taking a little bottle of rack, which I always carry about me, poured some down his throat; in fine, I brought him to life, and she and the maid, her servant, assisting, we brought him into this little wood to which we are going, a place which I had chosen to make me a little oratory in, and had caused my converted savages to build with some boards, making me a kind of little chappel with an altar, and a small chamber or dormitory behind it to repose in in the heat of the day.

Here I used to perform the holy duties of my office, to baptize, and give the blessed Eucharist, having under the altar a way into a little vault, where I keep poor vestments and what else belongs to the altar. I brought them to this place, fearing the jewels she had on, and her beauty, might tempt the savages to some wickedness: for should the savage Prince Manca, who governs this part of this barbarous country, hear of or get sight of this fair European, he would have her for his brutish pleasure in spite of all entreaties or resistance; therefore I secured her here, where she has remained a whole month concealed. Her adventures, and the brave Gomez her husband's, you shall know from themselves: in this place and company I will leave you, and at my return to your companions, tell them a wild beast came out of a wood and devoured you, so send them away by the first opportunity, and then I will disguise and conduct you, Elvira, her husband and servant, to Cartagena, from whence we will go together for Europe, or where you please; for I am weary with living amongst savages, and having but a little time more to live in the world, am desirous to spend it in my convent amongst my countrymen and friends, who may lay me to rest when dead amongst my ancestors. The hardships I have endured for twenty years in this place, have so broke my constitution, that I am not able to hold it much longer.

By this time they were come to the wood, and so ending their discourse, the monk presented Belanger to Gomez and Elvira, who being acquainted with his adventures, embraced and welcomed him to their poor habitation, overjoyed that they should have such company, and promised to go with him to Virginia, and procure him all the satisfaction he could desire of the governor of the island of St. Domingo, Elvira being the vice-roy's daughter.

But words cannot express Belanger's surprise at the first sight of these strangers; he thought Elvira so beautiful, that she excelled all her sex; her air, her shape, dress and face, and the gloominess of the place she was in, filled him with an unusual veneration and respect for her. Gomez was tall, finely shaped, and had a majestic sweetness in his look that commanded the respect and gained the love of all that saw him. Their servant was a young Indian maid, who though of an olive complexion, was very agreeable, well shaped, and had eyes so black and shining, that it was dangerous to look upon them.

The monk used to send them provisions by this girl, whose name was Philinda, having been christened by Elvira, who took her when a child, and had brought her up. Philinda went every morning to the hut to fetch such poor food as the monk could procure for them; they drank water from an adjacent spring, had some poultry that they kept in the wood to supply them with flesh and eggs, there being plenty of fowl in those parts, as likewise roots: the country being not very well peopled, they lay on straw; and there growing very good grapes in the valleys, they had hung some up to dry in the sun upon the hedges, and squeezing the juice out of others, drank of it instead of wine.

Thus these great people, who had been used to all the delicacies in nature, and had never slept but upon down, and used to have the finest clean linen every day, were now content to live in the poorest manner, and found that it was possible to live without all those things that a plentiful fortune furnishes.

The monk having thus introduced Belanger, and stayed some time with them, took leave; and then Belanger being entreated, entertained them with a more particular account of his life and adventures.

After which Gomez returned the favour with the relation of his and Elvira's, being seated under a fine spreading tree near the door of their cottage, it being now the close of the day, and a fine evening, Philinda being near them milking two tame she-goats which the monk had sent thither, and which were of great use to them.

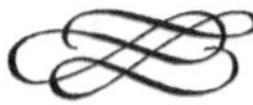

Gomez began his relation in these words: "I should first relate my dear Elvira's birth, and speak of her family. She was the only daughter of the Marquis of Mirandola, who is descended from one of the noblest families in Italy, though born a Spaniard. Her mother was Elvira Mariana de St. Briente, daughter of Don Lopez, Lord of Langora, a Castilian lord of great merit and fortune.

The Marquis, being a great favorite of the King of Spain, was appointed Viceroy of the Indies in the year 1692, at which time Elvira was thirteen years of age. He arrived safely at Mexico the same year with all his family and has resided there ever since, which is now ten years. I am the son of Don Alvares de Mendoza, an Aragonian lord, a man of equal birth and fortune with Elvira's father; but there was a mortal hatred between our two families, owing to a fatal accident that happened in my infancy.

My father had a sister, esteemed one of the fairest and most accomplished young ladies in Spain; she was but fifteen when my father brought her to court. A young Castilian cavalier, colonel of the guards and nephew to Elvira's father, saw and fell in love with my aunt, who was already promised to a lord of the first quality and fortune in Aragon. He courted her privately by means of a servant who was in his interest; and having gained my aunt's affection, at length obtained the last favor.

It was not long after this unhappy converse that the lord to whom she was promised arrived, and she was constrained to marry him. He, suspecting her virtue—being sensible she was not a virgin—became furiously jealous, yet concealed his thoughts from her and all the world, resolving to wait until he discovered the happy rival that had been before him, before letting his resentments break forth. For these reasons, he gave her opportunities of seeing her lover, carrying her down to a country seat not far from Madrid, which he had bought since his marriage, under pretense of obliging her, but indeed with the design to discover the fatal secret.

Here he often left her for a night or two while he stayed at Madrid with the king. The unfortunate Don Duante (her lover) failed not to supply his place in her arms, going disguised to a peasant's house in a village nearby, from whence, attended only by one servant, he entered the gardens and went into her apartment by a ladder of ropes, which she used to fasten for him on a balcony opening into her chamber.

Her lord (the incensed Aragonian) soon discovered all, by means of a page he had employed to watch. One night he concealed himself in a summerhouse in the garden, having only this page with him, both well armed; and the moon shining very bright, saw Don Duante go into her chamber by the ladder, which he left hanging for his retreat as usual. He stayed until he supposed they were undressed and gone to bed; then he mounted the ladder, followed by his page, and coming into the chamber, where a wax-light was burning on the table, approached the bed softly.

Don Duante, having heard some noise, started up and sat upright in bed. This gave Alonzo a fair opportunity for his revenge, and he stabbed him to the heart with his dagger; the poor lady shrieking out, he tore her out of bed by the hair, cut out her tongue, and, discharging one of his pistols in her face (which he had loaded with small bird-shot on purpose), left her on the bed blind, her eyes and face in a dreadful condition, all torn to pieces and full of shot.

Never was there a more tragic scene than this chamber: she looked like the wronged Lavinia, and the unfortunate Duante lay weltering in his blood, expiring on the floor. Thus one imprudent, sinful action occasioned the ruin of three noble, accomplished persons; nay, involved their families in the greatest misfortunes, and has entailed them on their posterity. The first ground of which was the lady's parents, who, not consulting her inclination, matched her against her will; want of firm virtue in her made her yield to another, when she was engaged by them; and an unchristian spirit of revenge governed her husband and made him commit two dreadful murders, incurring the anger of Heaven and the justice of laws—though he escaped by flight and his prince's favor, yet it ruined his peace and fortune.

I hope it will be a warning to all who hear this dismal story to avoid the like crimes. The distracted Alonzo, having discharged his fury, thought of his own safety, and taking some gold and his wife's jewels out of a cabinet in the room, descended the ladder, and, attended by his page, went out by a gate other than that by which his rival had entered. Mounting his horse, which he had left there with his page, they rode away as swiftly as possible to a place twenty miles farther, where he took shelter in a convent of Benedictine monks.

Don Duante's gentleman, finding his master stayed longer than usual, grew uneasy and, quitting his horse, ventured up the ladder, thinking he might be asleep. But entering the room, he was filled with such horror and amazement that he alarmed all the servants with his outcries. The poor lady was not dead; she was such an object as would have excited compassion in the heart of a barbarian.

It was easy to guess the cause of these dreadful deeds, had the gentleman not revealed them by his lamentations over his dead lord; but he concealed nothing in his passion, but too well explained the lady's crime and his master's. Not to stay longer on so sad a subject, a surgeon being fetched, the poor lady was put into bed, and her face dressed; but there being little appearance of recovery—which indeed would have been a greater misfortune to her than death—her confessor was sent for, who prayed for her and gave all the spiritual comfort he could; and though she couldn't speak, yet by signs, she testified her repentance.

He stayed with her many hours, till, finding the anguish of her wounds and loss of blood took away her senses by a strong fever, he left her to the care of her servants and assisted Don Duante's gentleman to remove his master's body into a hearse the servants had brought to carry him to his own house at Madrid. Then he returned to the lady, to whom he administered the last rites of the church, and about four in the morning, she expired.

I need not tell you how enraged my father, and all our family, were against the cruel Alonzo when this story was known; nor were Don Duante's friends less afflicted. But Alonzo's family did all possible to obtain his pardon of the king, pleading the enormity of her crime and the justice of his procedure, insisting he could do no less than sacrifice both her and her paramour to repair his honor; that the injury was unpardonable in both; that the cruelty he had exercised on his lady was excusable, considering the provocation. In short, they said all that could be in his defense, while her family and Don Duante's used all their interest against him, and were so potent that, though the king was inclined to forgive and only banish him, he deferred to declare himself, giving time for him to escape with much wealth, having sold off and conveyed his estate before process could be got out against him. However, he was sued and condemned when he was out of reach of the law.

My grandmother broke her heart for her unfortunate daughter. Elvira's family and mine, though they joined in prosecuting Don Alonzo, yet conceived a mortal aversion to one another, and much blood was spilt on both sides by duels and rencounters. A few years later, the king honored her father with this great post in the Indies, to prevent further effusion of blood and quarrels.

I was too young at the juncture when these misfortunes happened; but Elvira and I, growing older, my soul was charmed with her beauty; and though I could foresee no hope of gaining hers or her father's consent, I could not forbear loving or desist from pursuing her. My quality and fortune made way, and having nothing to urge against me but a family difference, the charming Elvira, consulting reason and religion, saw the folly and injustice of that procedure, and gave ear to my persuasions. At last she generously confessed a passion for me and promised to be mine, provided I could gain her father's consent.

Then I applied to my father, who, acquainting the king with our mutual affection and pleading this was the only way to reconcile the families and end that fatal strife which had such ill consequence, prevailed with his Majesty to propose it to Elvira's father. But he delayed giving a positive answer, having before obtained the viceroyalty, and departed without it, obliging me to follow. I obtained a letter from the king, in which he even commanded Elvira's father to give me Elvira and let our marriage be at once consummated. My family and hers all joined in this, and I departed Spain with a whole packet full of such letters.

I was certain not to be refused now, since he did not dare disoblige or disobey the king. I arrived safely at Mexico, was well received, and soon after married my dear Elvira. Now, being completely happy, we studied how to divert ourselves and take all the innocent pleasures of land and sea. Being at a pleasure-house of the governor's on the lake, we boarded a yacht one evening to take the air on the sea, it being fine weather, and resolved to spend the night in mirth and pleasure.

Several ladies and gentlemen were with us, with music. We supped, danced, and were merry; but about midnight a terrible storm blew up, and after being tossed many days and nights, not knowing where we were, we were driven upon a bank of sand near this shore. Here we lay bulging till the yacht was torn to pieces, then every one shifted for himself. Elvira and our friends reached the boat; I placed myself next to her, resolving to bear her to shore if possible, in case the boat did not make it in the storm—as happened, for it was soon swallowed in the waves.

I caught hold of her, bidding her throw her arms about my neck, and, it being day, made for the shore which I saw before me. But my strength being spent before I could reach it, just as I felt land under my feet I fainted; she, laying hold, pulled me up and saved me.

Philena, having got hold of a plank that was floating from the ship, to which she clung fast, was by Providence saved; and the wind blowing directly to shore, she was thrown on the sands before us. Seeing my distress and Elvira's, she ran to her assistance, who otherwise would have perished with me. They dragged me on shore out of the reach of the waves, and there the good Father came to our relief.

Thus divine Providence has preserved our lives and yours in a miraculous manner, and will, I hope, furnish us with means to return to our homes in health and safety.

Thus Don Gomez de Mendoza ended his relation, and they passed a few days as agreeably as the dismalness of their abode would permit, the Monk visiting them every day, when the savages were gone fishing. One evening the Monk, returning home, saw some white men, who appeared to be Europeans by their habit, sitting round a fire boiling a pot on the shore; their fire-arms, being muskets, lay by them. He saw that a pinnace lay on the shore, and discerned a ship lying at anchor about half a league off: he made signs to them to permit him to come near; they answered, and he hastened to them, and found they were come from the island of St. Christopher's, and bound to Spain.

He told them of the Spaniards he had saved, and prevailed with them to take them on board their ship; so he went and called them, and they were overjoyed to get away, and meet with such a lucky opportunity; and the Monk thanked God that he was rid of them, being uneasy while they were on that shore, lest they should discover his concealed friends whom he dearly esteemed, but these he abhorred as being villains. They went away that night, returning many thanks to him, and seeming very sorry that Belanger was not still alive to go with them; but hoping in themselves, as it afterwards proved, that when they got to the island of St. Domingo, the revengeful governor would reward them highly, designing to tell him that they had disposed of him in the woods, where he had been devoured by the wild beasts.

The glad Monk carried the good news of their departure to his friends the next morning. And now they consulted about getting to Carthagena; by land it was very dangerous, and by sea very difficult;

for they had the savages to fear as they traveled, and dreadful mountains and woods to pass through; and no boat of strength sufficient to carry them and provisions enough for a voyage of so many days at sea; and, what was worse, no pilot to guide the vessel if they had one. In fine, they knew not what course to take. At last they resolved to venture to cross the great river Oroonoko in the savages' fishing-boat.

This being resolved, trusting in Providence, they prepared to go; but the night before they were to depart, they saw a man running down the adjacent hill, pursued by a fierce tiger: he had a drawn sword in his hand, and a strange-fashioned coat made of beasts' skins; he had no shoes or stockings, but pieces of bear's skins tied about his legs with twigs; his head had a strange fur cap on; his face they could scarce distinguish, till coming into the wood, he climbed up a tree, and the beast, pursuing him to the foot of it, Belanger, who had fetched a gun, shot it dead, having perceived the man was a white, and his countenance no Indian.

No sooner was the beast killed, than the man leapt down from the tree and ran to embrace his benefactor, whose surprise cannot be expressed when he saw his face and heard him call him by his name, and knew it was the honest Captain of the ship who lived at Virginia and had carried him and his friend Montandre to the island of St. Domingo.

Elvira and the brave Gomez, who were retired at the stranger's approach, hearing them talk, came forth and invited him in, being together in the hermitage, for that was properly the name of their cell. They asked him to eat—a favor he gladly accepted of. Philena set what provisions they had before him, such as cold fowl, goat's milk, bread, dried grapes, and water, and wine made of their juice—a noble feast to a man who had lived for above five weeks on roots and fruits, such as the woods produced, and had not tasted any dressed food, neither bread, meat nor fish.

. . .

BEING MUCH REFRESHED, he related to them the manner of his coming thither:"I was going on a voyage for some merchants," said he, "to Barbadoes, about six weeks ago, my ship being heavy-laden with goods for that place, at which I was to unload and take in others for other islands. I had a fair gale of wind and good voyage till I came near the Summer Islands; then a storm arose and drove the ship up this river, where it was dashed to pieces against some rocks, among some unknown, and, I suppose, uninhabited islands. I had but eight men and a boy aboard, two of whom were blown off the shrouds into the sea: those that were left got out the boat and we quitted the shattered vessel, which was full of water above the first deck, and committed ourselves to the mercy of God.

The night was dark as pitch, and we knew not which way to steer. At last the boat, unable to hold out against the dreadful waves that bore her up to the sky one moment, and then opening, seemed to sink her into the bottomless deep—the wreck being filled with water by a great sea that washed over her—sank; and then we gave ourselves over for lost, and were all separated, never to meet again in this world, I fear. Nature taught me, though hopeless, to struggle for life; and it being just break of day, I discerned the shore, and made for it; the wind sitting fair, helped me greatly.

At last, I reached it half dead, and sitting down on the side of a rock to recover myself, looked round to see where I was, and soon found I was cast on this inhospitable shore, where I must expect to be devoured either by men or beasts; this made me almost repent that I had escaped drowning. I had no arms nor food, and my soul being full of horrible apprehensions of the cannibal-savages, I sought a place to hide myself and, looking about, crept into a hole in a great rock, not far from that on which I sat down; and being spent with the fatigue of the past night, I fell into a profound sleep, out of which I was awakened some hours after by two savages, who were stripping me and had already got my shoes and stockings.

But as they went to pull off my coat and waistcoat (which they could not do without lifting me up), I awoke, and looking up, caught one by the throat and, wrenching this sword out of his hand, he broke from me, carrying away my clothes, which he held so fast that he tore off my coat and waistcoat as he broke away, and they both fled with incredible speed. I was now left almost naked, and fearing they would return with more savages and fall upon me, I fled up into the woods, not knowing where else to hide myself but amongst the trees and bushes; and now, being ready to faint with hunger, I searched about for wild fruits and roots, and ate whatever I could find, which, alas! instead of satisfying my hungry stomach, made me sick.

I sat in a tree all that night, and the next day, as soon as it was light, crept down to the shore to see if I could espy a boat or any of my sailors, hoping they might have escaped like me; and there, to my great surprise, I saw my boat lying on the sands, and was transported to find her there, thinking I might get off with her the next tide and reach some of our islands. So soon as the water flowed and the sea, coming in, set her afloat, I ran down and leaping into her steered by the rudder along the shore. But I found I was not able to govern her at sea: I wanted strength and more hands, had neither oars nor sail, yet feared to lose her. Finding I could not venture out, I resolved, if possible, to secure her where the savages should not find her, in hopes that I might meet with some Christians here, by chance, who, like me, had been cast ashore, and would as gladly escape as I.

I brought the boat accordingly along the shore, till I came to a kind of a creek so covered with trees that it was almost impossible to perceive anything that lay there. I brought her in at the end of this creek, where was a thick wood. Having hauled her ashore, I broke down green branches and made a kind of bower over her, so that she lies well covered, and I have lain aboard her every night since. I have every day ranged about for food, living chiefly on the eggs of sea-fowl and turtles, which I found in the rocks and on the sands; nor did I dare to attempt to make a fire to dress anything, for fear of discovery; so I sustained life by sucking them and eating turtle raw, laying the flesh in the sun till it was hot, and then eating it as savorily as if it had been the greatest dainty. I knew not what to do for clothes; but one day, finding two bear cubs in the wood, I killed and flayed them, hanging their skins on the hedge to dry; these I made into the strange coat I have on: I killed some young goats also, and made a cap and spatterdashes, as you see.

But I must now acquaint you with the most surprising accident that ever befell a man. One morning, roaming in a wood, I met with a young woman fair as Venus but pale as death; she was wrapped in a piece of sailcloth, having nothing underneath but a fine Holland shift, a white dimity petticoat, and waistcoat; no headclothes but her hair— the finest light brown—down to her waist, all hidden under the canvas wrapper. She seemed half famished and so surprised at the sight of me, supposing me a savage, that she ran away as fast as she was able.

I followed her till she ran into a cave, and I entered and, getting hold of her, spoke in English asking who she was and her nation. She seemed most surprised and begged, 'Pray don't kill or be rude to me; I am a poor unfortunate maid, who by cruel guardians was trepanned and sent away for Jamaica; but our ship, being driven here, was wrecked, and I with a young man, the Captain's kinsman, were saved. Here we lived together for three days, but on the fourth, going out for food, he never returned and is, I fear, murdered. I have lived in this dismal place two months all alone under the most dreadful fears, almost famished and pinched with cold, not daring to go far from my cave for fear of savages.'

I was charmed by her face and pierced to the soul by her condition. I told her my story, begged her to come live at the boat, promising to protect her, to do her no rudeness, and to provide food as I could. She, with some difficulty, yielded; so I conducted her to my bower, and we have lived together three weeks. I left her two hours ago, and going out for food, met the wild beast you killed, fearing to return lest he follow and fright her, or find food near the boat and surprise her. By God's providence, that brought me here. And now with your leave, I will go fetch my dear Lucy, whom I have promised to make my wife on a Christian shore."

"You shall keep your promise," said Belanger, "tomorrow; we have a worthy Christian priest who will marry you. Since you have a boat able to carry us all, he will furnish us with provisions enough for a voyage to one of the Summer Islands, from where we may get a ship to Virginia, and thence to whatever place we choose."

The Captain hastened to fetch the lady, who in less than an hour reached the hermitage, joyfully received by Belanger, Gomez, and Elvira, who had never before seen anyone in such attire as her canvas shroud—a habit which ill suited her beautiful face and charming mien.

After eating together with thankful hearts, as much transported at this meeting as if they had forgotten their misfortunes, they lay down to sleep on straw, having recommended themselves to God, and rested sweetly, having no load of guilt on their consciences but minds resigned to the disposal of all things.

Next morning, the Monk visited them and was entertained with the history of the new guests, whom he immediately married, saying, "My children, it is not fit you should live in sin; and since necessity obliged you to live together, and closeness ensued, it is fit you should be joined by the holy bands of matrimony, that blessings may attend us all." And now they thought of nothing but preparing for their departure. The Monk informed the honest savages, whom he offered to take along, and they executed his commands with such alacrity, he was surprised.

In three days they got out the boat and victualed her, carrying on board boiled fowls, salted fish, bread, and fresh water in jars. The savage and his son made oars, well understanding the management of a boat, and fastened their fishing boat to her, loaded with provisions. They were perfectly skilled in the river's turnings and rocks, knowing every inlet and bank of sand; but out at sea, the Virginia captain would guide them. All ready, the joyful Christians went aboard, the women and children lying down in the boat covered with boughs. The Monk, Belanger, the Captain, and the savages rowed and steered.

They made sails with what the savages provided, passed safely out of the river, and at sea steered for Barbados. In a few days, with a fair wind, they reached Barbados. They were well received by a merchant friend of the Captain, and soon got passage to Virginia, taking

Gomez, Elvira, and Philena, who could get no ship to Mexico owing to war.

In Virginia, Belanger received the agreeable news that Montandre had sent a bark with letters for him from himself and Charlotta, telling him the governor was dead, and that they designed to sell off all their effects in St. Domingo and come to Virginia, leaving only Charlotta's two children behind, whom her husband's friends would not part with. He was so transported, he could scarcely wait for her coming.

But four days after, she and Teresa, with Montandre, arrived with an immense treasure. Never was there a more moving sight than the meeting of these three persons; Belanger, clasping Charlotta, stood motionless, as if he meant to die in that posture, and his ravished soul would fuse with hers; his eyes fixed on her face, big tears escaping while love sparkled in his eyes, as if the flame within sent out those crystal drops.

She hung upon his neck and cried, "Do I live, and again see Belanger! Blest God, it is enough." Montandre, meanwhile, woke them from their rapture: "My friend, my kinsman, have you forgot me? May I not claim a second embrace after Charlotta has received your first?"

At this, Belanger turned and caught him in his arms: "My dearest friend, next Charlotta, you are dearest to me. My obligations to you are so great, I cannot express my gratitude, nor could my whole life suffice to repay you, though wholly devoted to you and her."

Old Montandre and his lady interrupted them—or they'd have hugged forever. Belanger was so impatient for happiness that he would not rest until Charlotta consented to marry him that night; and the Monk accordingly wedded them, and they were mutually pleased. For what greater satisfaction can mortals attain, than to possess the person they ardently love, especially after so long a separation? This is a pleasure only lovers know; eternal bliss is contained in this: to possess all we desire and all worthy our affections; and, while we are mortal, nothing equals the joy of possessing the one we love.

Gomez and Elvira shared in their friends' happiness and were glad to stay some months with them, with the Monk, who resolved to go with Belanger and Charlotta to France, they offering to provide for him so long as he pleased to stay. During their stay in Virginia, they lived very agreeably; old Montandre and his Lady, still fond of Belanger, entertained them nobly, and Charlotta, now a sincere Roman Catholic, prevailed with the Monk to be her chaplain and to stay with her always.

They took all the diversions the place afforded—walking, riding, dancing, and feasting. One evening, Charlotta entreated the Monk to share the adventures of his life:

"Certainly," said she, "they must be very extraordinary, since you have passed through so many countries." He smiled, and replied, "Yes, Madam, I have met with many strange accidents, and am ready to oblige you and the company with the relation; nay, I will own my weaknesses, and give you the history of my youthful follies."

They all sat down under the shade of some trees by a little brook where they were walking; and, all silent, he began his narrative thus.

CHAPTER 21

I was born in Valladolid in Spain. My father was a Grandee of a
noble family, but having been refused a post at Court, to which
he believed himself to have a right, he too freely spoke his
thoughts, and gave his enemies an opportunity to traduce him to the
King, whose favor he lost, and so retired in discontent to his own seat
at Valladolid. I was all the children he had, and designed to be the heir
of his honors and fortune.

I was a student at a college, about sixteen, when it was my misfortune to see a farmer's daughter, whose beauty made me her captive. I
stole out alone into the fields behind her father's house every evening
for a month together before I spoke to her, and there saw her playing
with the lambs, and feeding the young goats; her plain dress and innocent behavior made her look more charming in my eyes than gold and
diamonds; her beauty and modesty were irresistible, and I loved her
to distraction.

In fine, I spoke to her, told her my passion, and found her wit and
apprehension exceeded her face and years. I succeeded according to
my wishes, gained her love, and resolved to marry her; but being not
old enough to be master of myself, and having no fortune in my own
power, I was forced to defer doing it till I was of age, and had got

some settlement in the world: for these reasons I pursued my studies with great application, resolving to be a physician or lawyer, that I might soon be able to provide for myself. In the meantime, I promised my dear Leonora to maintain her as my wife, and accordingly paid her father the half of the pension my father allowed me for her board, bought her silk petticoats, ribbons and laces; so that I half starved myself, and grew very penurious in my own expenses to provide for her: and she soon grew to be so fine, and so like a lady in her air and behavior, that the farmers' daughters, and other country maids envied her, talked loudly of this strange alteration; which, with my continual visits at her father's, though I thought none observed me, confirmed their suspicions of her being a mistress to me.

This report soon reached the principal of the college's ear, and he had me watched, and sent my father word, who immediately sent for me home, and schooled me sharply, commanding me to declare the truth; on which I ingenuously confessed my engagements with Leonora, and declared boldly that I would marry her or die. This so enraged my father, to see his ambitious hopes thus crossed in me also, that he proceeded to threats; in short, he was very severe with me, put me into the hands of a rigid tutor, who kept me as a prisoner ever in his sight.

I was now eighteen, and fancied myself a man sufficient to manage myself. Leonora's father was threatened, and turned out of his farm and livelihood by my father's instigation, who was a true Spaniard in his resentments. Poor Leonora, who was now looked on as the ruin of her family, was drove to despair. She sent many letters to me, but none came to my hands; my father intercepted them all. She, and her poor father and mother were retired to a village twenty miles further, and had there got into a little farm where they could just get bread.

I fell sick with the distraction of my mind, and was like to die; but youth and medicines recovered me, or rather the Providence of God, which reserved me for other uses. So soon as I was able to creep abroad, I went into the fields with my cruel tutor, and resolved to try to make my escape, let the consequence be what it would; but knowing that without money I should be no ways helpful to Leonora, or be able to travel far without discovery, I consulted what course to take, and at last concluded to rob my cruel ambitious father, whose strong box was never without a good sum of gold in it; it stood in a closet in his chamber, and it was impossible for me to get at it but by going in at the window from the garden.

I revolved in my mind many days what to do, before I could resolve on my course; at last I thought of an expedient, which was this: My tutor lay with me, I plied him with wine at supper, so I rose in the night when he was fast asleep, clapped a gag in his mouth, tied his hands and feet with my garters, though not without much struggling and some noise. For though I had made all ready before I went to bed, and fastened his hands to the bedpost before he stirred, yet when I went to tie his feet, he waked, and opening his mouth to speak, I clapped the gag, which was a piece of hard wood, between his teeth, stretching his jaws sufficiently; yet he roared strangely, till I threatened to kill him with my pen-knife, which silenced him, for he was a great coward.

Then I got down from my chamber-window by a vine that grew against the wall; and finding a ladder which the gardener always left in a greenhouse, the door of which I broke open, I set it against my father's closet-window, and went in, taking the strong box, which was not above two foot and a half square, but very heavy. I hasted down with it, and set the ladder against the garden-wall, which I got over, and stood some minutes consulting which way to go; and considered that if I was taken, my father would not hurt me farther than to chide and lock me up: I was but weak, and could not go far, so I made towards a river, where there used to be a ferry-boat constantly, thinking to offer the old ferryman, who knew me, a piece of gold if he would carry me over, and convey my box for me to some town where I might get a disguise, and a horse to carry me to Leonora's father's, whose removal to the poor village I knew nothing of.

It was about two o' clock in the morning when I left my father's, and a very light moonshine night, nor was it above three miles to the ferry; but I was so weak, and the box so heavy, that I was three hours before I reached it. I found the old man just launching his boat; he lifted up his hands at the sight of me, I knew it was in vain to dissemble with him, so told him my story: the good old man's heart melted with my sad tale, he condemned my father, pitied me, and offered to serve me faithfully on my promise not to let my father ever know of it.

And I have made it my observation, that there is more compassion and true friendship amongst the vulgar (said the good father) than amongst the great; for they are so engaged in their own private interests and designs, and so much at ease, and unacquainted with misfortunes, that they have very little sense of other people's, and forget that they may at one time or other stand in need of a friend themselves; whereas the meaner people, who are sensible of the miseries of a low condition, and daily meet with disappointments, have a great deal of compassion, and readily assist others.

This good old man wept at my story, carried me over, and, leaving his boat in his son's care, went with me to a fisherman's cottage, where he dressed me in old boots, the man's old coat, a thrum cap and worsted mittens like a poor fisher boy; then he engaged the man to go along with me wherever I pleased, fearing his going with me himself would discover me; and now being to pay him, I knew not how to open the box, and had no money about me; besides, carrying the box was the ready way to betray me.

I therefore resolved to break it open, and empty it, and throw it into the river, which I accordingly did, and was greatly surprised to find two thousand pistoles, and many gold and silver pieces of foreign coin and medals in it, besides all my dead mother's jewels, with her picture set round with brilliant diamonds, and the chief deeds of my father's estate; in fine, enough to make Leonora and me completely happy in a humble retreat. I paid my old ferryman to his content, disposed of the money and other things about me, sewing the jewels and writings into my clothes, and posted away with my guide to the town where I had left Leonora; there I was informed of what had befallen her father, and where they were gone to live.

I hasted thither, and discharged my guide before I went to the house, sending him back with the horses he had hired to bring us; and then entered the poor cottage where she was, in so great a transport of joy, that running to her as she was sitting in a chair at work, I fell down in a swoon at her feet; she had not time to know me before I fell, but yet did not fly from me, but lifting up my head to help me, saw my face, and giving a great shriek, fainted; her mother coming in at the door, saw us both lying on the floor, and crying out, waked me from my trance: I rose and embraced her and my reviving mistress.

I told them in few words how I got from my father's, and what I had brought; that my design was never to leave Leonora any more, but to live and die with her. And now the good man being called, we all rejoiced at our happy meeting, and consulted what was next to be done; it was altogether improper for me to stay there but a day, for there my father would be sure to look for me, and where else to go or how to part with Leonora on any account, I could not resolve; at last the good man proposed to me to go to a Benedictine monk who was his confessor, and trust him with the whole affair, and ask his advice and assistance; he was a man of singular integrity and vast experience, a person of noble birth and great years.

I consented to this proposal; we went to him, he received us kindly in his cell; and after giving me some gentle reproofs for my undutiful-ness to my father, finding me resolute, and determined to marry Leonora, and fearing, I suppose, that if he refused to do that office for us, we might live together in a sinful state, he at last consented to my desires, and promised to serve us in all he was able.

He sent me to a widow-lady's house five miles thence near Soria, who was his aunt, and sent Leonora's father to fetch her thither also; in the evening he came to us, and that night I was made possessor of that lovely virtuous maid, whom I at his request suffered to return home with her father the next morning, on condition that she should return to me at night; this we did with design that if my father sent, they should find her there, which would induce them to believe that I was not yet arrived, and would divert their pursuit of me for some days, and give us time to get over the Pyrenean mountains into France, whither we were resolved to retire.

All things succeeded as we expected; about noon officers came to search my father-in-law's house, examined him and Leonora, her mother, and their man and maid, who all pretended ignorance; and finding they could get no satisfaction or intelligence where I was, they went away. This Leonora gave me an account of at night.

Father Dominic, the good Benedictine, provided us horses and a guide for the next morning, and gave me letters of recommendation to several priests and persons of quality in Gascony, advising me to settle at or near Béarn.

My dear Leonora and I, returning a thousand thanks to him and the lady, took leave; I presented the father with twenty pistoles as a present for his convent, gave three amongst the lady's servants; and being both dressed in men's clothes like servants in livery-coats, being some of the lady's servants' clothes, we departed. I had given Leonora's father a hundred pistoles, and agreed that he and her mother should come to us so soon as Leonora and I had taken a house, and were settled. We had very fine weather and a safe journey, though much fatigued in passing the Pyrenean mountains: and having presented my letters to the persons to whom they were directed, I was received by them with such civility, and so treated, that I was amazed, and no ways repented my leaving Spain: the gentry and clergy seemed to vie who should be kindest to us; the ladies courted and treated Leonora so highly, that she soon became as free and unaffected as they were, and so improved, that I thought her every day more charming.

So soon as we arrived in France, I sent back our guide and horses, with letters to the good old father, the lady, and my father and mother-in-law; on the receipt of which, Father Dominic wrote to my own father, acquainting him that I was married to Leonora, and gone out of the kingdom, that I was extremely sorry he had constrained me to leave him in such a manner, and was willing to return to him, if he would forgive me, and receive my wife into favor; in fine, he urged all he could think of to reconcile us, and received an answer, by which he found my father was implacable, and so incensed against me, that it was in vain to hope for any accommodation between us, at least for some time.

My father and mother-in-law came to us, and having taken a pretty house and some lands, he managed our little estate, and my wife and I kept the best company in the province, and lived at ease; it did not please God to bless our marriage with any children, but everything else prospered with us.

I wrote often to Father Dominic, sending him presents of what I thought might be acceptable, particularly wine, of which I had enough, having now bought a little vineyard: he sent to my father to let him know that I was well, and longed to visit him, but for seven whole years could never perceive by his answers that his displeasure was abated. All this while he never acquainted him where I was; at last my father falling sick, relented, and sent to him to send for me, and that I should bring my wife along with me.

I no sooner received this joyful news, but I made ready to go to him; and leaving all to the care of my honest father-in-law, my wife and I, attended by two servants, set out for Valladolid, where we soon arrived, and were received by my father with much tenderness.

But alas, my oversight had drawn him into another; during my absence, he had taken a young handsome kinswoman into the house and debauched her; this was a secret could not be long hid from me: she was saucy and insolent to my wife, which I resented, and desired my father's leave to return to France; he desired me not to leave him any more, and would know the cause of my disgust, and who had offended me: at last I modestly told him, our pert kinswoman took too much upon her; he colored, and said it should be remedied; but, as I afterward discovered, he had two sons by her, and knew not how to get rid of her: this made her insolent, and finding I had made my complaint to my father of her, she was fired with revenge, and resolved to destroy my wife, who was now to my inexpressible joy with child; she disguised her thoughts, seemed sorry for what she had done, and so behaved herself, that Leonora, who was all goodness, forgot what was past, and grew kind to her; but the viper ill returned it: for drinking chocolate one morning together, she put poison into my dear Leonora's cup, of which she languished about a month, and then died; the physicians were of opinion that she was poisoned, and when she was dead, I had her opened, and was too well convinced of it.

My affliction was so great, that I was inconsolable. I suspected my father, and could not believe his strumpet dared to have committed such a deed without his knowledge and consent. I seized her, and had her examined before a magistrate, but she denied all, and I had no proof of the fact; so I took leave of my father, having had some sharp words with him, and returned to France the most disconsolate man living.

And now I had time to reflect on all the actions of my past life, and too late became sensible that my disobedience to my father first drew God's anger upon me, who had accordingly punished me in bereaving me of her who had been the occasion of my sin, and was in some kind culpable herself, though more excusable than I, yet had paid her life for her fault. That my father, who had been too severe, and ought to have had more indulgence for my youth, and less ambition, was punished by the divine justice in being permitted to become a slave in his age to a vile passion, no ways just or honorable like mine, and blasted his fame.

These considerations inclined me to quit the world, and dedicate the remainder of my life to God, being then but twenty-nine years old. I accordingly settled my affairs in France, leaving my father and mother-in-law in possession of my estate there, taking only for my own support a thousand pistoles and my mother's jewels, which I had still reserved, and ordered my estate to go to a convent in the town where it lay near, after their decease; and taking my mother's picture, and the writings I took from my father, set out for the Benedictine convent where Father Dominic lived. I acquainted him with my design, he approved of it, and then I waited on my father to obtain his leave and blessing.

There I found the wicked Isabella, my father's mistress, had been her own executioner, having gone distracted with the remorse of her conscience, and so had cut her own throat, having in her madness discovered all the circumstances of the murder she had committed on Leonora. My father was so struck with the manner of her death, and shame, his crime with her being now made public, that he seldom went out of his chamber.

Our meeting was at this time very different from our parting; I fell at his feet with the greatest submission, and with tears begged pardon for the follies I had committed in my youth; he wept over me, and lifting me up, embraced me, unable to utter one word: then his countenance expressed the confusion of his thoughts; he blushed at his own weakness, and could not look me in the face: at last he said, "My son, we have both offended God, but I more grievously; God pardon me, as I do you." A tender conversation ensued, and we passed some days together in pious discourses, I hope much to our advantage.

I begged him to make some provision for the two unfortunate children he had had by this ill woman, and settle his affairs, as I had mine; he told me he would be wholly directed by me. In few days he fell sick, and continued ill for six months: having in that time settled his affairs, by my desire the estate was given to his nephew, a worthy young gentleman, with several legacies to his poor relations and the church; he expired in my arms with great piety and resignation. I buried him nobly, and then retired to the convent, where I lived many years, being received into that fraternity.

At forty years old I was chosen by our superior to be sent to Peru, and from thence went amongst the people where you found me, among whom I endured great hardships, it being long before I could acquaint myself with their language and barbarous customs; yet the austere life, and good I did them in curing their sicknesses and wounds, with my discourses of God and Christ, so wrought upon these savages, that they listened to me and revered me. I was several times taken prisoner by different parties of these barbarians, who are ever at variance with one another; but they still spared me, having a notion that I was a holy person.

Those I converted to Christianity were very hard of apprehension, and yet very devout when once instructed. I had lived seven years with the poor fisherman and his family, whom we have brought with us, and was doubtless preserved by Providence to be the means of your deliverance: and now I hope to spend the remainder of my days in that pleasant country where I was once happy with my dear Leonora, whom I might still perhaps have enjoyed, had we never left it; but it was Heaven's will that I should be what I am, and therefore won't repine.

Here he ended his relation with a deep sigh, all the company being much pleased with the manner of his relating it, and the strangeness of his adventures; admiring the wisdom of God which had preserved him amongst savages, and placed him where he was the means of their preservation.

CHAPTER 22

Gomez and Elvira, with Philena their faithful slave, having hired the bark that brought Charlotta and her dear friend and sister to Virginia, arranged to carry them to the island of St. Domingo, and from there to Mexico. Having made Charlotta and Teresa presents of two rich jewels—part of those Elvira had on when she was cast on the barbarous shore—and making great acknowledgments for all the favors received, they took leave, promising to continue their friendship by a constant exchange of letters. They added that, if they ever returned to Spain, they would make a tour to France on purpose to see them. For Charlotta and Teresa had contracted so great a friendship, that the latter had made her husband promise to settle in France, his religion being no hindrance, as he was a subject of England, having been born in Virginia, and therefore had nothing to fear.

As for Belanger, he was persuaded by his wife and the monk to be a Roman Catholic, which was the faith in which he'd first been raised. Gomez and Elvira returned thanks to old Montandre, his lady, the captain, and Lucy, and all who had visited and treated them, offering to serve them all in trade or otherwise, whatever was in her father's power. They departed with a fair wind and arrived safely in Mexico, as was later reported by letters from them and considerable presents received some months after, by the same bark that carried them.

Young Montandre, who had received a great fortune with Teresa, agreed with his father—who had other children by his young wife—to take a certain sum of money, to be remitted in goods to France as his fortune. He began to prepare for their journey there, where Belanger and Charlotta longed to be.

The poor savages were settled in old Montandre's plantation, he having given them a little house and ground to live on, at his son's and the good monk's request. A ship being got ready and loaded with their effects, Charlotta and Teresa, with their husbands, went on board. There, they took leave of the good old gentleman Montandre and his lady, with the honest captain and Lucy—the fair maid he had made his wife—who, hearing part of Charlotta's story, had concealed her thoughts to this moment. When going to take leave of Charlotta, after a noble entertainment which Belanger and Montandre had given them on board the ship, Lucy threw her arms about Charlotta's neck, saying,

"I cannot part with you, Madam, before I reveal a secret to you that nearly concerns you: Are you not the daughter of Monsieur du Pont, who lived near Bristol and married a second wife from London, by whom he had a daughter named Diana? And were you not trepanned to Virginia by that mother-in-law?"

"Yes," answered Charlotta, much surprised. "I am the daughter of that unfortunate gentleman, and was by that wicked woman betrayed and exposed to a thousand misfortunes. But who are you? For I am impatient to know."

"I am," said she, "that daughter, Diana, and your sister by the father's side—by the justice of God for my mother's sins, doubtless, exposed on the seas, and more barbarous lands; but by His mercy saved, and honestly disposed of to this generous man," turning towards the captain, her husband.

All the company, but especially Charlotta, were impatient to hear her story. When all were seated, she related it in a few words:

"My unjust mother, having got rid of you—whom she made my father and the world believe were drowned coming back from the ship with her and Captain Furley—applied herself wholly to amass a sum of money to provide for me and herself, resolving to return to London and pursue the same unhappy course of life she had before followed, which I am too much confused at the mention of to explain further: for her shame is in some measure mine, though I bless God I have never been guilty, but ever had an aversion to all wicked actions.

In order to accomplish this design, she took up clothes and money from everybody that would trust her; and in a short time, my father was persecuted on every hand and unable to raise money fast enough to satisfy his creditors' demands. You may imagine that this caused a great many quarrels between my father and mother, but she minded nothing he said, continuing her extravagances so long that at last he was arrested by Captain Farley, who pretended that she owed him a hundred pounds by a note under her hand; and, having before mortgaged his estate, it was not easy for him to get bail immediately.

The night he was taken to the officer's house in custody, my mother packed up the plate and linen, and all that was worth carrying away; and, taking me, went aboard a hoy bound to London, which Furley had provided, and left my father. What has become of my poor father since, I know not; but I fear he is—if alive—in very bad circumstances."

At these words Madam Belanger wept; and her husband, wiping away her tears, kissed her and said, "Come, my dear, be cheerful; you and I will fetch him from England, and take care of him. If he is dead, being a good man, doubtless he is happy, and does not need our help."

DIANA CONTINUED: "Being arrived in London, my mother went directly to Westminster to her friend Miranda's, but found her gone from the house, and well married to a sea-captain, with whom she lived happily and honestly in Portsmouth, as the old bawd informed her, to whom she went seeking information. So she took a lodging in the bawd's house, and soon got a rich gallant—an old merchant of the city. Though she was still very handsome and had very rich clothes, she was now in years, and not of an age to attract the young fops and rakes.

I was about eight years old when she went to London; and, doubtless, she intended to advance me to be some great person's mistress, or some rich fool's wife. She had robbed my father of nearly two thousand pounds, but Furley peeled her of a good deal of it. She kept me very fine, carried me to the parks, the plays, and had me taught to dance, sing, and play the spinet: in short, she took pains to make me agreeable but none to instruct me in virtue and goodness. Yet God had given me the grace to abhor her way of living; and I often wept for her sins in secret, and wished myself in prison with my good father, or, if he was poor and at liberty, that I might beg for him rather than be a mistress.

In about two years' time, in which we had changed our lodging at least ten times, and my mother had ruined two or three merchants and a linen draper, she was struck with sickness, and rheumatism took away the use of her limbs, so that she lay a long time unable to help herself; then she broke out into boils all over: in short, she became full of ulcers and died in a most miserable condition, to my great grief—I fear little sensible of her sins and destitute of all spiritual help, having only the vile old bawd about her, and the people in the house where we lodged.

After her death, everyone plundered something; and though she had made a will—though no widow—which she left in the tally-man's hands (her old acquaintance), he and Captain Furley were her executors and my guardians. The tally-man came and buried her privately, and indeed poorly, and carried me home to his house, Furley being gone on a voyage to Ireland. I know not what my mother left me, but believe it was considerable, as she often told me she could give me a handsome portion.

I was but meanly treated at this vile tally-man's and, being ready to break my heart, begged day and night to be sent down to Bristol to my father—but that was not his nor Furley's interest, for they well knew my father would call them to account for my mother's effects. Old Gripe told me, as soon as Furley arrived, they would consult what to do with me; accordingly they pretended to send me to my father, but, putting me into a wagon, sent me to North Wales, to a place where I could hear nothing but Welsh, and lived four years miserably —all the while unable to escape to Bristol, having not a penny nor anyone to help me but poor ignorant people.

At last, being now fourteen, I applied myself to the parish minister and told him my story. He was a very good man, and wrote up to London to a friend, whom he ordered to find out the tally-man, to threaten him, and try to find what they designed to do with me and what my mother had left me. This gentleman did so, and Gripe laid all the fault on Furley, promising to send for me to London, which he did immediately. At my arrival, he treated me kindly. Then Furley and he contrived to get rid of me for good and all; so they appeared mighty ready to send me to my father, and went with me on board a ship that lay in the river, bound—as they pretended—for Bristol, and ready to sail. They had bought me new clothes and given me my mother's watch, and, being young and ignorant, I didn't suspect their villainy. Furley pretended he would go along with me, and the tally-man gave me a broad piece at parting and left us at Greenwich; but Furley went with me as far as Sheerness, where, pretending to go on shore about some business, he left me, and I never saw him more.

I knew it was a great way to Bristol by sea, yet was every hour asking when we should get there, and how far we'd come. But a young man, the captain's nephew and a very honest youth—took pity on me and told me, 'You are not going thither, but to Jamaica: he heard his cruel uncle bargain with my cursed guardians to carry me thither, they have paid your passage and he has promised not to sell you, but to get you a good service; but be assured he will strip you of all your clothes as soon as he reaches Port Royal and sell you for a slave.'

I thought I would have died at this news, but the young man begged me to take no notice of his telling me; 'for if you do,' he said, 'I am undone, my whole dependence being upon my uncle, and he will discard me.' I told him, in return for his trust, I would keep his secret. Then I told him all my story, and how these villains had wronged me with my fortune, and that if he could help me escape anywhere in England and go with me to my father, I would give him any part of my fortune he should fairly desire, once it was recovered. He answered that he had other terms: I should promise to marry him if he delivered me, and then he would free me out of their hands, even if we had to go to Jamaica, as he feared we must, being past land and out at sea; 'so soon as we land, I will go to the governor, swear you were trepanned, and tell him all; my uncle is there, and will take my part; besides, if you marry me as soon as I can get you ashore, he cannot sell you.'

I CONSENTED TO HIS PROPOSAL, thinking any honorable way to escape the miseries ahead should be accepted; moreover, if I refused, I would surely be ruined in Jamaica by some villain who would buy me for vice and force me to comply. After this, Mr. Stephen (for that was his name) studied how to oblige me, taking such care that even though there were two wild young men—sons of merchants—aboard the ship, he engaged an honest gentlewoman, a passenger, to keep me in her company always; and I went very safe.

But nearing Jamaica, our ship was driven up the River Oroonoko and shipwrecked, as you have before heard related—and there this unfortunate young man, I fear, met his death by the hands of barbarians, whose virtue and piety deserved a better fate. As for myself, I have made a choice much more to my liking in my dear husband," turning to the captain.

Charlotta ran and embraced her, saying, "Dear sister, our fates resemble each other so much, I am astonished at the Almighty's justice. Be assured, if I ever live to see England again, I will see justice done both to you and our dear father." At these words, the old captain bowed and saluted Charlotta and Belanger, saying, "I think myself very happy to have such worthy relations, and doubt not but you'll assist my wife in all things whose virtue I am convinced of; and as I took her without the prospect of a fortune, I value her no less though she never have any." They all persuaded him to take his wife and go along with Charlotta for France and England, but the good man, being in years and having a plentiful fortune in Virginia, did not care for further hazards. So they took leave, and went ashore with old Belanger, his lady, and the other friends, and the ship set sail the next morning and, in ten weeks, arrived safely at St. Malo.

Belanger was joyfully surprised with news of his guardian's death and that Angelina and his sister, with her husband Monsieur Abriseaux, had safely arrived in France by way of Spain; that Angelina was healthy with Monsieur du Pont, and that Du Riviere—who had long before left Virginia—was now living with his reconciled Louisa.

Charlotta's arrival and his was soon spread abroad; and not many days passed before they and all their friends sent or came to congratulate them and invite them to their homes. In a few days, the now most happy relations and friends met all together at Belanger's house, who was now possessed of his estate, his sister having received hers before his arrival. They entertained one another nobly and shared accounts of the strange adventures they had all met with.

Monsieur du Pont, having retired in despair of ever seeing his dear Angelina, recounted the manner of their meeting thus: "I was sitting by a fountain in my garden when a servant came and told me that two ladies and two gentlemen in a coach insisted they must speak with me—perfect strangers, he said, and I denied them, saying I was busy and would not see company; but they would not be refused, and one lady said she would see me though I were dying. At these words I rose and flew to the gate, where my Angelina was standing without; but no words can express the transport I was in at seeing her. I caught her in my arms, ran into a parlor with her, and, setting her down, sometimes gazed upon her, then kissed her, saying and doing I knew not what, nor did I remember my kinswoman and Monsieur de Abriseaux were present, though they stood by, or Monsieur Morine the surgeon, who all laughed—but at last Angelina reminded me of our friends, and I welcomed them in a few words. Indeed, I was so distracted to know Angelina's adventures that I kept her from sleeping with my questions half the night."

Just as he spoke, Monsieur Riviere and Louisa entered. Belanger and Charlotta saluted Louisa.

"Dear kinswoman," said he, "I sent your wanderer home to bless you with his presence, and repair the injuries he did you."

"Indeed," said she, "when he came to the gates of the convent to ask for me, I could hardly credit my eyes, he was so changed; but I soon threw aside my veil and fled to his arms with as much affection as at the first months of our marriage."

"You are," said he, "all goodness, and I beg you make no more mention of my crime, since I hope God and you have forgiven it."

"Where is your son?" said Belanger.

"At home," said Monsieur du Riviere, "well, and such a one as merits a better father than I: he'll be here soon to wait on you."

Many days passed in visits and entertainments, too tedious to recount. But after some months, Charlotta being big with child and Madame Montandre near her time, Charlotta continually importuned her husband to go with her to England (it being the year of peace between King William and France); but he feared to venture her upon the sea in that condition and offered to go himself. Madame Montandre also would not part with her before she was brought to bed. "My dear sister," said she, "will you leave me now, after coming so far out of affection, leaving my own country and relations for you? Can you consent to leave me?" Thus, Teresa was delivered of a daughter, and Charlotta of a son two months later; and, not able to leave for two months more, at last, being recovered, Charlotta and Belanger sailed to England from Calais, and landed safely at Dover.

They hired horses to Bristol, where few knew Charlotta, but she learned her aged father was in prison, ruined for debts wickedly contracted by his wife. She would not stay a moment but flew to the prison, winged with filial piety and tender affection. She asked for him so earnestly, the jailer was startled; but slipping him half a crown, he let her in. She soon saw her dejected father, creeping along in rags, his white beard long to the leather girdle of his coat. He lifted up his eyes, fixed before on the ground, as she said, "Sir, let me speak with you"; seeing a fine lady and gentleman, he put out his withered hand, expecting alms, having no notion of her being alive. She was in such disorder that Belanger, fearing she would swoon, drew her aside. Tears streaming down her face, her voice faltered, she could hardly speak—only clasped her arms about the old man's neck, crying, "My dear father," and fainted.

These words caused a tumult in his soul; he trembled, held her fast, and gazed upon her, unable to speak. Belanger, moved by the sight, could scarcely restrain his tears. Gently taking the old man's hand, he said, "Sir, be not surprised, God can do wonders. There's a mystery in my wife's words, which if you collect your spirits a little, we will explain." The old gentleman, staring, cried, "It cannot be! 'tis all wonder, 'tis my child's face, 'tis her voice, and yet—" At these words, he dropped down. Belanger called for help; two or three prisoners came, their ragged faces and poor habit testifying to want. They lifted Monsieur du Pont to a poor room, where his bed lay on the floor, and Belanger carried Charlotta, now recovered, after him. He called for wine, gave some to the old gentleman; after which they talked and wept together. Charlotta deferred telling her tale until they were out of that woeful place, sending the jailer for his creditors; but as this took time, she paid the entire debt—just three hundred pounds —into a merchant's hands, and took him home, the merchant indemnifying the jailer. At the merchant's, they refreshed and reclothed the old gentleman, who wept for joy and praised God so passionately all present were moved to tears as well.

His creditors came, pretending sorrow for their actions, but he and Charlotta treated them with such scorn as their unchristian conduct deserved. Now all his friends and old acquaintance came to visit and congratulate him; those that had helped him in prison she entertained splendidly, and, lastly, sent to release the five poor debtors who had shared his cell—their combined debts amounting only to £120—a noble gift which earned her their blessings.

Having supplied herself and her father with all they needed from England, Charlotta, her father, and Monsieur Belanger returned to St.

Malo in the same vessel. The old gentleman, now so ancient and long absent as to need fear nothing for his religion, resolved that if ever molested, he would remove to Jersey or Guernsey, whence he could pay or receive a visit from his daughter.

Angelina recounted her incredible adventures in Barbary, which filled them all with admiration. One morning—a French ship having entered the port in the night—an old man in a poor habit came to young Monsieur du Pont's house, asking to see Angelina. She was at breakfast with her husband and bid the servants admit him; but was amazed when she recognized the face of the old French captain who had carried her to Canada.

"Madam," said he, "I have come to beg your pardon before I die; God has seen fit, by a harsh slavery, to punish my sin. At last, in His mercy, He has granted me return to my native land. Yet I could not die in peace until I knew what became of you. Having heard last night that you were alive, I hastened here, also to seek your favor for two Christian strangers who escaped with me from Tunis—a gentleman and lady, lately slaves, with nothing to support them upon landing or to carry them home."

Monsieur du Pont and Angelina assured him of their forgiveness, and said they would be glad to assist the strangers in anything. Du Pont said, "I can hardly forgive you what you did concerning my wife, but as a Christian, I won't resent it—bring the innocent strangers and we will help them." The captain took leave, and an hour later returned, bringing a gentleman and lady. She was very handsome, her shape, stature, and mien delicate and engaging. The gentleman was tall, slen-der, with a face so lovely and majestic that he seemed the offspring of Mars and Venus, though both were meanly dressed, being recently freed slaves.

Angelina embraced the lady, saying, "Welcome to France," though she knew not if she understood. The gentleman addressed Angelina: "Madam, you wonder why my wife and I come first to you; but when I say her name is Silvia de Mount-Essaigne, formerly your companion in the convent and much honored with your friendship, you will not wonder." At these words Angelina ran and embraced her, and

Monsieur du Pont cried out, "Then you are my dear school-fellow Charles du Bois! My God, where have you been all these years, and what providence preserved you, whose death I have mourned so passionately? Sit, and tell us all your story, for we must not part again —my house and fortune are at your service."

Angelina cried with Silvia, both so overwhelmed with joy they knew not what to say. At last Monsieur du Bois began to relate their strange adventures.

"You know," said he, "that my father dying while we were schoolfellows, I was left in the hands of two rich East India merchants, Monsieur Dandin and Monsieur du Fresne. Dandin had but one daughter, who was as deformed as Esop and as ill-natured as she was proud and ugly. My fortune was very considerable, and his whole aim was to match me to Magdelain, and so secure it to his posterity.

I was but thirteen, and he wheedled me into signing a contract with her; and she being twenty, was not a little pleased to have such a fine young husband. She took much upon herself, and so tutored and schooled me upon every occasion, that my aversion daily increased towards her. I was forced to hand her about to every place she was pleased to gad to; and at last it was my fortune to go with her to a chapel near the monastery where you and my dear Silvia were pensioners. There I saw you and her together: you I knew, because my friend Monsieur du Pont had shown you to me; for students always tell their amours to one another, and I am younger than he, so that he had a mistress before me.

I was so charmed with her, that had not my fury been along with me, I had followed you to the convent; but I soon found an opportunity to go there and found you gone. I got to speak to her, and in some time gained my charmer's consent to marry me secretly. She, you know, was an orphan, who, being related to the abbess—your aunt— was bred there with design, having but a small fortune, to be made a nun. Being but a pensioner, it was no difficult thing for her to come to me; but my keeping our marriage a secret until I was of age was hard enough. My guardians did not keep me short of money, so that I fancied I could easily maintain her if I could but get some faithful friend for her to live with privately in the house with his wife and family, or else a private lodging.

This last I thought most secure, and accordingly took a chamber in a widow-woman's house in a village. Having thus provided a retreat and engaged my confessor to marry us, I gave her notice, and she got out the next morning with another pensioner, on the pretense of going to church at the little chapel I had seen her at. I waited for her in a coach near the chapel, and coming out in the crowd, she slipped from her companion and, turning back into the church, went out at another door, where I took her into the coach and drove away to the friar's cell, where we were married. Thence we went away to the village, to our lodging, where I had provided a dinner and all things for our reception. The widow's daughter, a very modest young maid, I had hired to wait on her.

Here I stayed all night, having pretended to old Dandin, my guardian, that I was to go out of town with a young gentleman whom I kept company withal, and whom I had trusted with my secret and engaged to ask me to go with him before my guardian and Magdelain, my crooked rib that was to be. In fine, I kept my dear Silvia here some months, though a great search was made after her, being very cautious in my visits. She was in that time with child, but miscarried. She never stirred out of doors without a mask, and when I fetched her out in a coach; but finding it was inconvenient to have her so far off, I removed her to St. Malo's and took a lodging for her at a widow's house in a back street, in a very private place, with a garden, and a back door into the fields.

In this garden Silvia used to walk, and would sometimes look out of her windows into it. A young lord who often passed by that way saw and fell in love with her. He soon inquired who kept the house, and learned that it was a widow who had a young gentlewoman and her servant lodged with her. Emboldened by his quality and fortune, he went to the house in a chair, richly dressed, and asked to see the lady, the young gentlewoman who lodged there. The woman, seeing his attendance and habit, was daunted. He asked no leave, but going by her, went upstairs and found Silvia sitting in her chamber reading. She was surprised, but he told her his business was love, and in fine would take no denial, or be gone. He supposed her a mistress by the place she resided in, being so mean and obscure, and resolved to possess her whatever it cost.

She told him she was married, but he turned that into ridicule. Before he went he presented her with a fine diamond ring, which she refusing, he left it upon the table. He went not away till midnight; the next morning I found her in tears, and she told me what a misfortune had befallen her. I was now but seventeen, and the expense of maintaining her and a servant so sunk my allowance that I had no money by me; and being something indebted to the widow, I knew not how at present to remove her.

In fine, this young nobleman, who was mad in love with her, continued frequently to visit her, and set spies to discover who kept her, who soon got knowledge of the secret. This young lord, one of the most powerful persons and with the greatest fortune in the place, knew my guardian and sent privately for him, telling him, as out of friendship, the matter.

"Monsieur Dandin," says he, "you have a young heir contracted to your daughter who will be ruined; he keeps a mistress in such a place. 'Tis your duty and interest to put an end to such an intrigue and save the youth from being undone." My guardian promised never to reveal who told him, and returned him a thousand thanks; so he came home, took no notice to me, but watched me the next time I went out and dogged me to Silvia, and at my return home, told me I must go travel or marry his daughter next week.

I was ready to go distracted before, but now I was quite overwhelmed. I found I was watched and did not dare go to Silvia. The next morning when I was in bed, he entered my chamber, searched my pockets, took away all the money I had left with my watch, and told me, "Young gentleman, I am informed you keep a mistress. Your allowance shall be shortened; you are like to prove a good man and an excellent husband, that begin so well."

I was so enraged I lost all patience; I told him I would never marry his daughter, and that as soon as I was of age, I would call him to a strict account. I know not what I said, but we quarreled so that I rose and went out of the house, protesting I would never set foot in it again. I went directly to Silvia, but cannot express the transport of sorrow I was in when I came there and found the poor widow and the maid in tears, who told me that at twelve o'clock the preceding night, somebody knocked softly at the door. They supposed it to be me; and the maid, rising and going to it, asked who was there. Somebody answered, "It is I, du Bois;" at these words, she opened the door and a man in a vizard caught hold of her, clapping a pistol to her breast. Three more rushed in, all masked, and ran upstairs, dragging Silvia out of bed; she saw them bring her mistress down, bound hand and foot, and put her into a chair. One man stayed till the chair was gone, as they supposed, a good way; then he bid her shut the door and make no noise, for if she did, he would come back and kill her.

The poor creature was so frightened she had not the power to stir for some time; at last she went up to the widow and acquainted her with what had happened. This was all I could learn, and enough to make me desperate. I returned to my guardian like an enraged lion, demanded my wife, declaring my marriage: this made him as furious as I; he threatened to sue me for the contract with his daughter. I applied myself to several of my relations and friends to assist me against him, but nobody cared to meddle, for he was known to be a very rich and a very cunning man. Then I challenged the young lord, charging him with stealing her, but he only laughed at and ridiculed me.

At last, being unable to get any news of her, I resolved to travel, believing they had murdered her. I was deeply melancholy; and my guardian, who indeed knew not what was become of Silvia, was willing to be rid of me and readily agreed to my traveling. I designed to go first to Rome, then make the tour of Europe, and return to France as soon as I was of age, to be revenged on my guardian. He agreed to make me a handsome allowance and gave me five hundred pistoles to defray my extraordinary expenses, being willing to be reconciled to me before the day of reckoning came.

Attended by a servant, I set out on my journey, reached Rome, having viewed all that was curious in my way through Spain. I resolved to stay there some time and took a lodging for that purpose. One morning my servant waked me, saying there was a youth, who said he came post from France to me. I bade him call him up; when he entered my chamber, he made a sign with his hand that I should send away the servant. I did so, and then he ran to me and caught me in his arms. But good heavens! how I was transported at that moment when I saw it was Silvia.

I shut the chamber door, and then she told me that being (as I knew she was) pretty far gone with child, the fright had thrown her into such a condition that when the villains who had carried her away came to take her out of the chair, she seemed half dead; they carried her upstairs into a chamber richly furnished and laid her upon a bed and so left her. The young lord came in immediately and told her that she must now consent to his desires, that he would never part from her again. That it was in vain to resist or call out for help; in fine, nothing but the condition she was in preserved her; for telling him she was in labor and would die if he did not call somebody to her assistance, begging him with tears to pity her condition, she prevailed with him to defer the execution of his brutish design, and he called an old woman and her daughter to her.

She had no other help but these women; and, falling into a fever, lay sick in her bed for three months, unable to rise; all which time the young lord continually visited her, bringing a physician several times. At last, recovering enough to walk about her chamber, she began to consider how to escape. By this time, as she afterwards learned (for I had declared our marriage), the young lord refrained from visiting her some days.

One afternoon he came, and being alone with her, he said:

"Silvia, I am come to ask your pardon for the injuries I have done you; I thought you a mistress, not a wife, and my passion for you was so excessive, it blinded my reason. I believed you ruined by a man already engaged, not half so able to care for you as I. Had you been a virgin, I would have married you, but finding you are virtuous and

Monsieur du Bois's wife, I am heartily sorry for what is past, and ready to restore you to him. He is gone to Rome in discontent. As soon as you are able to travel, I will furnish you with money and a servant to wait on you there. Believe me, Silvia, I love you no longer with an unlawful passion but with a tender affection as a sister. I will, as soon as your husband is of age, assist him with all my power against Monsieur Dandin, who has been the cause of all this mischief."

Here he revealed to her what had passed between him and Dandin, and how they had contrived together that he should steal her away and carry her to his country house, where the servants were in his devotion and supposed she was some young lady their master had gotten with child. Nor dared they inquire further. In fine, as soon as my wife was able to ride, she put on a man's habit by his advice; and, having received a thousand pistoles from him, set out for Rome, attended by one of his servants.

Nothing could be more welcome than she was to me, and I concluded that the disguise she had on was the best thing in the world to conceal her till I was of age and to prevent further misfortunes, which her beauty in a female dress might again occasion. I now wanted only a year and a half to being of age, and had no mind to return to France till that time was elapsed; so we removed to a lodging some miles from Rome, where Silvia, who passed for my kinsman, lived with me; we passed the time very agreeably.

At last we embarked aboard a vessel bound for Marseilles and set sail with a fair wind; but in a few hours, a terrible storm drove us out to sea, and we were driven for forty-eight hours before the wind, in which time our ship was so disabled that she sprang a leak; and had not a ship come up, we would all have perished in the merciless sea. But alas, it would have been better for many of us; for it was a Corsair of Tunis, belonging to a great Bassa there, and we were all put in irons and carried thither.

How inexpressible was my concern for my dear Silvia, you may easily imagine. At our coming ashore, we were brought to this Bassa's house, who, viewing the prisoners, selected her and me for slaves, supposing we were prisoners of birth and that he should have a large ransom for us. He inquired about our nation: I answered we were natives of France, and brothers, that we had been at Rome, whither our father, a private gentleman, had sent us and we were returning home. He seemed satisfied and treated us gently, making us write or attend him into the country, riding by the side of his litter. But I soon perceived he had a wicked design on Silvia, whom he dressed in fine Turkish clothes and treated with great indulgence. I was seized with dreadful apprehension at this procedure and resolved to risk everything to escape his hands. This led us to a plan which we happily effected.

The French captain who brought us home was at that time his slave; he had been so to the Bassa's father, a general who had treated him very cruelly. By his father's death, he fell into this Muly Melce's hands, who was a good-natured man, and finding him skilled in sea affairs, made him master of a neat pleasure-boat used for his own diversion. He also trusted the captain to take Algerine slaves out to fish for him. The captain was generally thus employed in the summer and much in his favor. I was often sent aboard with him, but Silvia never. I contracted a friendship with him, and we contrived our escape thus: he learned of the Christian fisherman and his wife where you had lived, directed me thither, and we agreed Silvia and I should retire there, which was not difficult as we could walk the town. He would send slaves ashore and bring the pleasure-boat around in the dusk of evening and take us in—all our hope was to get to Malta in this light vessel, a dangerous undertaking, but our condition made us resolve to trust in providence and venture all risks.

There was a lovely maid who had been sold to this Bassa some months before, named Margaretta des Sanfon. She, a farmer's daughter from Poicton, was a servant with a lady going with her family to her husband, a merchant settled in the West Indies. The ship was taken by a pirate of Tunis; she became a slave and fell into Muly Melce's hands. The captain had fallen in love with her, so sent her along with us to the fisherman's.

All was ready and the Bassa absent, being called to the court, so we got away. The captain came at the appointed time, and it pleased God that we arrived safely at Malta in four days, the Algerine slaves neither suspecting our plan nor interfering as we entered the port, they being only five in number and unarmed. Here we were received as Christians ought to be, and furnished with clothes and refreshments, having escaped with nothing but what we wore. From Malta, we got passage in a French ship that put in there.

Now, providence having brought us back to our own country, we must beg your assistance to get Dandin to deliver up my fortune."

"That," said Monsieur du Pont, "is easy, for he is long since dead, and his daughter is married to a very honest gentleman, Monsieur de Fontain, the banker, who I dare promise will gladly restore to you all that is your due." Angelina entertained them nobly, and the French captain, having married Margaretta, brought her to wait on her. In a few days, Monsieur du Pont managed the affair, concluded an agreement between Monsieur du Bois and de Fontain, who honorably paid him what moneys Dandin had in hand, and Monsieur du Bois entered into possession of all his fortune.

Thus, divine providence, by various trials and strange vicissitudes of fortune, proved the faith and patience of these heroic Christians, whom neither slavery nor the fear of death could make forsake their faith or mistrust their God. They were all happily preserved and delivered out of their troubles and at last brought home to their native lands. Charlotta, whose filial piety and extraordinary virtues make her worthy of the highest esteem, had the satisfaction of seeing her dear father die in peace, in a good old age; was blessed with an excellent husband and many children, fair and virtuous like herself; nor was her prosperity interrupted by any misfortune. The virtuous Teresa and Angelina and the rest were blessed with all earthly happiness.

THESE EXAMPLES SHOULD CONVINCE us how possible it is to behave as we ought in our own conditions, since ladies whose sex and tender upbringing made them less able than men to support hardships bravely endured shipwrecks, want, cold, slavery, and every ill that human nature can be tried with; yet we, who never feel the inclemency of foreign climates, nor see the faces of pirates or savages, are impatient at a fit of sickness or disappointment, tremble at a storm, and are brave in nothing but in daring Heaven's judgments. Let us blush when we read such histories, and, imitating these great examples, make ourselves worthy to have our names, like theirs, recorded to posterity.

FINIS

www.ingramcontent.com/pod-product-compliance
Lightning Source LLC
Chambersburg PA
CBHW030141010826
48973CB00002B/673